Breakout

Mickey Dole's gang have broken jail, killing and plundering in their bid for freedom and ranch-hand, Clem Shaw, joins a posse that includes a devious bounty-hunter and a reluctant lawman. As the hunt progresses, Clem realizes that the situation is not as clear-cut as he thought: not all his enemies are in the fugitive gang which is now divided amongst itself.

There will be more deaths and shootouts before Clem unravels the puzzle and finds himself on the wrong end of a gun.

Breakout

Greg Mitchell

A Black Horse Western

ROBERT HALE · LONDON

© Greg Mitchell 2011
First published in Great Britain 2011

ISBN 978-0-7090-9268-1

Robert Hale Limited
Clerkenwell House
Clerkenwell Green
London EC1R 0HT

www.halebooks.com

Typeset by
Derek Doyle & Associates, Shaw Heath
Printed and bound in Great Britain by
CPI Antony Rowe, Chippenham and Eastbourne

ONE

Sheriff Bill Gleeson was normally a cautious man, especially when guarding a desperate crew like Mickey Dole and his three henchmen. But he made one mistake and its consequences escalated disastrously.

It all started when a crowd of drunks in the Lucky Seven saloon decided that it would be a good idea to lynch the gang that had attempted to rob their town's only bank and had killed two bystanders in the process. A group of paid-off trail herders had arrived in time to thwart the bandits' escape plans and, after further gunplay and deaths on both sides, the outlaws surrendered. The following day there was talk of lynching, so Gleeson and his three hastily recruited deputies took what they considered to be the necessary precautions.

The sheriff placed two men on the street outside his office door and posted the third inside. Then, as the whiskey-fuelled situation began to look more serious, he went through the dividing door to check on the prisoners in the cells. He studied them as he walked down the corridor between the cells on each side.

Dole no longer looked the defiant outlaw who had reluctantly surrendered the previous day. He was pale and visibly nervous. His lined face showed fifty years of the weathering and a couple of days' growth of black whiskers was the picture of anxiety. Shifting his long, skinny frame to the front of the cell, he said, 'That sounds like a crowd gathering out there. I hope you ain't gonna let us get lynched.'

'They won't get you while I'm alive,' Gleeson promised. 'That's just some of the town no-goods. They make a lot of noise but none of them tried to stop you *hombres* yesterday. They'll find it mighty dry out in the street and will soon head back to the saloon. I have two extra deputies outside just to make sure they don't even reach the front door.'

Dole's cellmate, Jack Craig, then weighed in to the discussion. An insignificant individual who looked as though he would be more at home behind a store counter, he pressed his face to the barred cell door and whined, 'What if you're wrong? It's our lives at stake here.'

From the cell on the opposite side of the narrow corridor, Lew Barstow immediately saw the idea behind his comrade's frightened mutterings. Craig was a new member of the gang but had proved to be

6

tougher than he looked. Barstow gripped the bars with his massive hands and said in what he hoped sounded like genuine fear, 'You've gotta give us a chance, Gleeson. We're trapped here like rats.'

Then Gleeson made his last mistake. He turned to face the big outlaw before realizing that he was too close to the bars of Dole's cell. Realization of this came the hard way.

An arm swiftly encircled his throat, choking off the sheriff's gasp of alarm. Equally quickly a hand plucked the revolver from his holster. Cocking the weapon and pushing the barrel against the side of the lawman's head, Dole snarled, 'Keep quiet and hand over your keys.'

Gleeson offered no further resistance. He could only make the best of what he knew was a very bad situation. Reluctantly he passed back the ring of large keys that he had been carrying.

Jack Craig eagerly snatched the keys and, swearing under his breath, tried several in the lock before he found the right one. At last the cell door swung open.

'Don't forget us,' Barstow whispered. There was an armed deputy in the main office.

Craig hurried across the aisle and opened the other door. Barstow and Len Stirling quickly moved out and tiptoed to the connecting door, positioning themselves one on each side of the opening.

'Call your deputy,' Dole whispered to his prisoner.

'Go to hell.' Bill Gleeson had a strong idea of what was coming and had no intention of calling another man in so that he too could be murdered.

'That was your last chance.'

With the gun pushed against his prisoner's body, Dole squeezed the trigger. The shot was muffled slightly but the deputy in the main office heard it. He threw open the door and stepped through. Even as he peered through the haze of gun smoke and his shocked mind reacted to seeing the body on the floor, it was too late. Strong arms seized him from both sides, twisting his half-drawn gun from his grasp. Dole shot him at point-blank range.

As the man on the floor writhed in his death throes, Stirling, with the deputy's gun, followed his leader into the main office.

Alerted by the shots one of the outside deputies came back through the front door. He had a sawn-off shotgun in his hands but it did him no good. There was not even time to cock it. Stirling fired once and the man dropped with a bullet in his brain.

Barstow scooped up the gun, stepped over the fallen man, yelled defiantly through the open door and emptied one barrel into the startled crowd outside. Then he slammed shut the door and shot home the bolt.

The horrified would-be lynchers went into retreat, emitting a mixture of surprised, fearful and, later, angry sounds. The startled yelling became fearful again as Stirling stepped to a side window and emptied his revolver into the already fleeing mob.

Barstow laughed in delight and gave them the second load of buckshot. A couple of wounded men lay in the crowd's wake and another, slumped over a horse trough, was ominously still.

'Get all the guns and cartridges you can find,' Dole ordered. 'We're getting out of here before those jackasses get over their fright.'

A search of the office revealed their confiscated sidearms in a closet, a Winchester repeater with a box of ammunition, and a few shotgun cartridges. Quickly they buckled their familiar weapons into place and loaded them while collecting the guns and gunbelts of the dead lawmen and looping the belts over their shoulders.

Barstow replaced the fired cartridges in the shotgun and Dole levered a round into the firing chamber of the rifle. He glared around at the others. 'Now we're getting out. Grab any horses you can get. That pack of yellow dogs will run rather than stand up to us. Kill anyone who gets in the way.'

Clem Shaw felt little sympathy for the weary horse that he bestrode. It had spent most of the morning in strenuous efforts to get rid of him and there was no other way to teach it that bucking was hard work and not particularly enjoyable. Bert Anson's ranch had a surplus of good cow ponies going to waste and Clem had been hired to ride the buck out of some before they were put on sale. He would have preferred more regular ranch work but the ranches were not hiring with winter fast approaching. Indeed, he felt himself fortunate to have found this temporary job. He was young enough to still have his nerve but old enough to have seen the many tricks of which rough horses are capable. The work was risky and though he liked it he was realistic enough to know that it was a young man's game. Sooner or later he would have to settle down somewhere.

The pony had lost most of its excess energy but the ranch was still a mile away when he saw a rider galloping towards him. He recognized the distinctive Appaloosa colour of Randy Anson's favourite horse and there was no mistaking the tall, broad-shouldered rider with a face that looked as though it had been chiselled from granite. Randy worked on the ranch for his uncle and aunt whose only son had swapped ranch life for a law practice in Chicago. From the little that Clem had seen Randy was a serious, cautious type and it seemed out of character to see him riding so urgently.

The Appaloosa was in a lather of sweat when the rider hauled it to a stop. His face had lost its normally impassive expression, his bright-blue eyes appeared wide open and shocked and his voice seemed cracked and nervous.

'Clem. Come back to the ranch quick. There's been a raid on the place. Uncle Bert and Auntie Ruth have been murdered. The house has been ransacked.' He paused as if to regain his breath, then continued, 'I was on my way back from shifting some cows when I thought I heard shots. When I got there it was too late. A lot of stuff has been taken. The murdering swine tied my folks to chairs and shot them – killed them both in cold blood. There was no need for that. It's a hell of a mess back there.'

Clem was shocked by the news. Many questions were running through his mind but his horse was no longer fit enough to keep up with Randy's mount and he had no opportunity to ask them. His pony was still trailing by a hundred yards when they swept over a low rise. Below, in a windbreak of sheltering pines, was the ranch house with its outbuildings and corrals.

A strange buckboard with a pair of horses stood in front of the house at an awkward angle. Coming closer the riders could see that a wheel was caught on a gate post. The well-trained team were standing patiently, waiting for someone to release them. But they would have to wait a while longer.

Both riders jumped from their horses as they arrived and ran through the open front door.

Clem was not prepared for the scene he encountered in the front room. The horror of it struck him more than a physical blow could have done. The bodies of Ruth and Bert Anson, still tied to chairs, lay on their sides in pools of blood. Both had been shot in the head. All signs of a peaceful home had been replaced by absolute chaos. Curtains were torn down, drawers and closets were open and indications of hasty plundering abounded.

For a second or two he stood there in shock until his companion brought him back to reality.

'They ransacked the place. There's all sorts of stuff missing,' Randy muttered. His voice seemed to quiver with rage. 'I think they got Bert's cattle money too.'

'Cattle money?'

Randy explained. 'Before you came here Bert sold a lot of cattle. I know he made a couple of thousand dollars on the deal. He didn't trust banks and had the money in a tin cashbox. I've had a quick look around the place but can't see it. My guess is that either Bert was forced to tell them where it was or those killers found it.'

'You know the place better than I do, Randy, and would be the best judge of what was taken. The sheriff will need to know all the details. If you see what you can find out here, I'll have a look around outside.' Clem shook his head as if in disbelief. 'I never heard of hold-up men arriving in a buck-board before. I think we'll find horses and saddles missing as well. If you feel up to it I'll leave you alone here and see what I can learn from outside.'

'Go ahead. I'll have a good look around here.'

It was a relief to get out of the house. Clem looked around in the dirt. There were hooftracks and bootprints. Some had been made by Randy and himself and their horses. The tracks of someone in flat-heeled boots stood out because normally ranchers and cowhands did not wear them. He was not a skilled enough tracker to know exactly the number of raiders but guessed there could have been four or five.

His next task was to unhitch the matched pair of bays from the buckboard. They had been used hard and were coated with dried sweat. Their brands meant nothing to him as he was new to the area. 'If only you could talk,' he told the animals as he led them round the house to the corrals at the back. In one corral he found a couple of the ranch's riding stock and two strange horses, still showing the marks of hard riding. After removing the harness from the team horses, he allowed them to drink deeply before putting them in the corral with the others. He did the same with his own and Randy's mount, which by then had cooled down.

A search of the saddle shed revealed that two saddles and bridles were missing. The signs were there and it did not take an Indian tracker to discern that four raiders had arrived, two on horseback and two in a buckboard. Four men had left the ranch on horses.

The bunkhouse had been plundered and his few belongings scattered around. His saddle-bags and

13

Winchester carbine were gone, but otherwise he had little that was worth stealing.

He was on his way back to the house when he saw the riders descending the high ridge a quarter of a mile to the east. The sun glinted on rifle barrels that the two foremost horsemen had in their hands. They disappeared briefly in a stand of cottonwoods at the foot of the slope and when they came into view again they were headed right for the house.

Clem had seen enough. He pushed open the back door and found Randy looking at the ruins of what had once been a neat kitchen.

'There's four riders coming and by the look of them there could be trouble. Do you reckon that gang has come back?'

Randy loosened his six-gun in its holster. 'They're in for a hell of a shock if they have.'

TWO

Randy moved swiftly across the room and looked out of the window. He relaxed slightly as he recognized the riders. 'That's our neighbour Jud Harris and a couple of his hands. They have Maryanne with them too. They must have heard the shooting.'

The pair walked out on to the veranda as the newcomers halted before the building. The two cowhands, one in his twenties and the other middle-aged, had that same hard look as their boss. The leader was a large man with a short grey beard and an angry expression.

But it was the girl who caught Clem's attention. She was young, dark-haired and beautiful. The worn flannel shirt, dusty divided skirt, and crumpled black hat did not detract in any way from her beauty and, by way of contrast, might even have enhanced it. She sat on her sorrel pony with the easy confidence of a skilled rider. But there was a serious, almost angry expression on her face as she looked about. He briefly removed his hat to the lady, then remembered that his dark hair would be tousled and that it was many hours since he'd combed it. Hastily he jammed his battered hat back on his head but he seriously doubted that the girl even noticed him. All the newcomers' eyes seemed fixed on Randy.

Harris wasted no time on formalities. 'What's goin' on around here, Randy?'

'There's all sorts of trouble, Jud – real bad trouble.'

'And there's gonna be more when I find out just who was shootin' at my Maryanne. Was it you?'

'What are you talking about?'

The girl spoke for herself. 'I was on my way here to bring a dress pattern over for your aunt. Someone opened fire on me from the house as I came out of the trees over there. I got out before their aim improved. The person was hidden by the window curtain but whoever it was had a good try at shooting me.' She looked hard at the young man before her. 'Who was it shot at me, Randy?'

'I don't know, but you're lucky they missed you, Maryanne. There's been a double murder here. Someone raided the house while Clem and I were away. They killed Aunt Ruth and Uncle Bert. We've only just found them. The place has been ransacked.'

'Oh no. . . .' the girl gasped, and some of the colour went from her face. She shuddered and said

16

in a shocked voice, 'That's awful.'

Jud Harris also seemed stunned for a second, then he gathered his senses and snapped, 'Do you know what happened?'

'Get off your horses,' Randy said, 'and I'll tell you all I know. But it's not much. It's not a pretty sight in the house but you're welcome to come in if you want.'

Clem said, 'It might be an idea if the lady doesn't.'

Harris glared at the young cowhand in his dusty boots and worn batwing chaps. He was always a little suspicious of drifters. 'And who would you be?'

'I'm Clem Shaw. Anson hired me a couple of days ago to gentle some broncs he was going to sell.'

'You ain't from around here,' Harris accused, as though being an outsider was a crime.

'You're dead right there.' The hard edge to Clem's voice indicated that he had supplied all the personal information he intended giving. He was not in the mood to be answering questions from those who had no real right to ask them.

Dole had set a hard pace since leaving the Anson ranch, determined to increase the distance between his gang and the posse that would inevitably follow. He did not worry about the horses because, like Indian raiders, his men would steal the next lot of fresh animals that they encountered. None of their mounts was really fit but that did not matter. It was cattle country, and at ranches they would soon find replacements.

Len Barstow, however, did not share his leader's optimism. He was a heavy man and his horse was starting to feel the effects of the weight and the pace. 'We should slow down a bit, Mickey,' he told his leader. 'These horses won't last long at this rate.'

'They don't have to last long. There's sure to be another ranch within a few miles and we'll swap them. All these ranches have plenty of horses. A posse will have to ride hard to get near us and they won't be able to change horses when theirs wear out because we'll have taken the best of the horses as we go through. Right now we have to be like the Injuns when they raided. We open up a big lead first and then keep getting fresh horses while them that's chasing us has to nurse along the same, tired cayuses. Some of those posse members will be townsmen with businesses. They won't be able to afford to chase us for long.'

At the thought of pursuit Stirling looked nervously over his shoulder and said, 'The sooner we leave this place, the happier I'll be. We've left too many dead behind us. The law gets a bit narrow-minded about that.'

Craig was enjoying the relief that freedom had brought and gave a short laugh. 'Who cares? We have nothing to lose at this stage. What's a few more bodies now?'

'Cheer up, Stirling,' Barstow said with a laugh.

'They can only kill you once. Think how often you've been shot at and how rarely you've been killed.'

They were riding west into the foothills of the Rocky Mountains, ascending stony ridges, following paths made by mustangs and wild cattle. These led through thickets of oak, pine and cedar, opening out occasionally to grassy meadows where the riders disturbed deer and even a small herd of wild horses, as well as open-range, ranch cattle.

'This is where we can lose the lawmen for a while,' Dole announced. 'We're riding unshod horses and mustangs will be using these trails as well as us. At the right place we'll change direction and leave any posse to go exploring in those mountain valleys. We'll gain a couple of days on anyone who's after us.'

Stirling remained pessimistic. 'You jackasses are living in the past. We might outrun men on horses but we can't outrun the telegraph.'

'I ain't dumb enough to try,' Dole announced. 'Them talking wires are only around the bigger, more settled areas. There won't be any where we're going.'

'These horses ain't gonna last much longer.' Stirling remained unconvinced of the plan's soundness. 'This one of mine is starting to get sore-footed already.'

'Stop your griping,' Dale snarled. 'This is still cattle country and there's bound to be more ranches ahead. We'll get us some new horses soon.'

As the horsemen topped the ridge they saw ranch stock in the distance at the mouth of a grassy valley. A narrow wheel-rutted dirt road snaked away into the distance and, given the nature of the country, the men knew that it almost certainly led to other ranches, where they would be able to replace their hard-ridden horses. It went without saying that the faster they did so, the more they would outrun any pursuit.

Harris and his men followed Randy into the house. Maryanne had steeled herself to follow, but Clem said gently, 'Don't go in there, Miss Harris. It won't help the Ansons and it won't do you a lot of good either.'

'But they were such good friends—'

'I know, and they wouldn't want to see you upset or having nightmares. I hardly knew those folks, but what I saw in there will haunt me for a long time. If you want to do something, you could help me with the horses.'

Maryanne thought for a while, then accepted Clem's advice. 'I'm Maryanne Harris. I haven't seen you around here before.'

'Just call me Clem. I'm not from around these parts. I was just drifting through and the Ansons wanted the rough edges taken off some horses they were going to sell. I've only been here a couple of days. You might recognize the brands on the buckboard team that brought some of these killers here.'

'I only saw them from a distance, but they looked a bit familiar. Let's have a look at them.'

They walked round to the corrals. Maryanne recognized the horses instantly. 'They belong to Emma Hayes. She's the wife of the banker in Jackson's Creek. They're well known but I don't know where the other two came from. The killers must have stolen Emma's buckboard in town. They must have robbed the bank.'

Clem frowned, pushed back his hat and rubbed his forehead. 'I can't see bank robbers using a buckboard, but maybe a couple of their getaway horses were killed. There would be people in Jackson's Creek who saw them so I can't figure why there was any need to kill the Ansons.'

'Some people must just kill for the enjoyment of it. These same people tried to kill me and I would not have been a threat to them. They could have captured me and tied me up like they did the Ansons.'

'Think yourself lucky that someone wasn't very bright and wasn't much of a shot,' Clem said, 'because if they were smarter you would have been dead like your neighbours.'

Maryanne climbed up on the corral rails and looked along the road that ran in front of the ranch. Far out on the plain she could see dust rising. 'Looks like riders are heading this way. It might be the sheriff and a posse from town.'

'They took their sweet time about getting here,' Clem growled. 'Those killers would have a long start, and thanks to the fresh horses they got from here, they're getting further and further away every minute.'

'What happens now?'

'There are some of the Ansons' better horses in that pasture behind that little hill over there. The killers only took the horses I was getting ready for sale. None of them is as fit as our working cow ponies. I'll get one of these horses and run the others up into the corrals. The posse might need fresh horses. There's a good horse of mine with them. He's shod all round and has had a few days' rest on good feed. I'll need him.'

'Will you be joining the posse, Clem?'

'I reckon so. The sooner those murderers are run down, the better.'

Maryanne walked to where her well-trained pony was standing with its reins down. 'I can round up those horses and run them in if you just open the gates for me. It will save you taking out one of these poor, tired horses.'

'That would be mighty helpful,' Clem admitted.

The posse arrived while Maryanne was away getting the horses. Clem watched them as they filed into the yard in front of the house.

A tall, thin man rode ahead. He was dark-haired, in his early thirties, with a large moustache, a worried look, and a lawman's star pinned to his vest.

George Weatherby was unsure whether he should have been leading a posse but, as the town's only surviving lawman, felt it was expected of him. A couple of middle-aged, mounted townsmen rode behind him on fat ponies, whose appearance advertised that they, like their riders, had seen no hard work for a fair while. Like their leader, Max Hall and Con Brady would rather they were not there, but felt they should represent the citizens of a town still reeling from such a disastrous bloodletting.

It was the fourth man who caught Clem's attention. He was of average size with sandy hair, probably about forty with a beaky nose protruding from a small, pinched face. He had the narrow eyes of a sharpshooter and they darted about, missing nothing of the scene before him. His horse was a tall bay thoroughbred. The stranger wore two six-guns, carried a rifle in a saddle boot and had a sawn-off shotgun in a leather loop at his saddle horn. He could have been a law officer but sported no badge. He was obviously a man who lived by the gun, one of a type that would operate on either side of the law if the money was right.

The man with the badge halted his horse in front of Clem. 'I'm George Weatherby, a deputy from Jackson's Creek. Mickey Dole and his gang broke jail this morning. They killed Sheriff Gleeson and a couple of deputies, shot up the town, killed and wounded others and even stole a lady's buckboard. Have they been here?'

'They sure have,' Clem told him, 'and have added a couple more murders to their score. Get down and come inside. You're just the man we want to see.'

THREE

When Weatherby and his men saw the scene inside the house they were at first stunned, then enraged. Killing in the first frantic minutes of an escape was one thing but to murder two helpless prisoners was a particularly cold-blooded crime. Expressions of disgust and anger were flying freely but the two-gun man was unaffected and mostly silent as he looked around. It was almost as if he had seen similar sights before.

Clem waited outside to intercept Maryanne when she came from the horse corral but, by standing near an open window, he could see and hear some of what was going on inside. A couple of gleaming brass cartridge cases lying at his feet showed that the shooter who had fired on the girl had leaned out of the window to shoot. The empty shells had fallen out of the window as the rifleman ejected them. Being from the ubiquitous .44/.40 Winchester, they were easy to identify.

Randy saw Clem at the window and came across. 'We're getting a posse together, Clem. Can we count you in?'

'You sure can but I don't have a rifle. Those skunks ransacked the bunkhouse and took mine.'

'You can have mine. I can't go at this stage because of what has happened here but I might join you in a few days. Weatherby is going to let the folks in Jackson's Creek know where he is and what's happening every time he gets near a telegraph station. You're in luck. Vern Black, the famous bounty hunter, arrived in town just after the breakout. He'll be riding with you.'

Clem was not sure that Black's presence was a matter of luck. He did not personally know the man but he had a reputation as a ruthless man-hunter with little regard for anything but the rewards on the men he sought. He had a feeling, though, that Black's experience would not come amiss. Weatherby, by a series of indecisive statements and half-hearted efforts to organize his men, looked as though he was already out of his depth.

The posse, to Clem's mind, was too small and poorly equipped. Guessing that the residents of Jackson's Creek were of doubtful use, mounted as they were, he suggested to Randy that a couple of the posse horses should be replaced from ranch riding-stock.

'Is that necessary?'

'I reckon it is. Those killers grabbed the horses I

had been working from the corrals. They're not fit and all are unshod. Maryanne is bringing in our regular horses now. Some of them are shod and in hard-working condition. Weatherby's posse isn't very big and two of those straight-shouldered, mud-fat ponies from town will girth gall before the day's out. We can swap them now or lose two riders by this time tomorrow.'

Randy thought for a while, then said, 'You're right. Pick out a couple of reliable ponies, but don't give them our best.'

Maryanne had the horses corralled when Clem got there. About twenty animals of various sizes and colours were still churning up the dust in the enclosure. He took a catching rope from one of the posts and selected two reliable mounts, which he quickly transferred to a smaller pen. Both animals had been freshly shod and he checked that all shoes were in place and the nail clenches were tight. Then the pair walked back to the house together.

'Were you shot at from the side window?' Clem asked. 'I saw a couple of empty shells that had fallen outside.'

'That's right. I'm lucky that one of that gang is a bad shot. If he had waited until I was a bit closer I would have been killed too.'

'I wonder what will happen with the ranch now?'

'I suppose Randy will take over for a while, but the ranch won't go to him. The Ansons have a married son, a lawyer named Harry living in

Chicago. I guess the ranch will be his now.'

Jud Harris met them at the back door of the house. He still looked shocked by what he had seen. He said that his two cowhands, Bill Lyons and Casey Hopkins would be riding with the posse. 'Weatherby's going to need every man he can get, but I reckon I'll be more useful here helping Randy get things fixed up.' He turned to his daughter. 'Ride home and tell your mother what's happened. Then help her get some food together. The posse can make a slight detour and collect it as they go past. Black's sure he can pick up the killers' trail.'

Maryanne put the reins around her pony's neck and mounted. 'It's been nice talking to you, Clem. I'll see you again soon.'

'Thanks for the help.' He would have liked to say more but as he hardly knew the girl and her father was present, he thought it best not to get too friendly.

Tom Dibley was splitting firewood outside the kitchen of his parents' ranch when he saw the riders approaching. He was only fifteen but he was nobody's fool. Immediately he sensed something was not right. They were not riding in a group like regular travellers but were fanned out on a single front. Ominously too, he saw that they all seemed to be carrying long arms. They bore no resemblance to men on a peaceful mission.

'Pa,' he called. 'There's strangers comin' and

they don't look friendly.'

His father came to the door and glanced out. His curiosity was replaced by shock as he recognized a situation he had hoped never to see again. He had spent all his life on the frontier and Indians and outlaws had attacked their ranch on several occasions in past decades. 'Get in here, quick,' he shouted urgently. 'Run – *run!*'

The boy threw down his axe and sprinted for the house. His father grabbed him roughly, hauled him inside and slammed the door behind him. 'Get the other rifle and warn your mother to lock the front door. Don't show yourselves at the windows and shoot anyone you see trying to get in. Get moving.'

As he spoke, the rancher snatched down the Winchester rifle from where it hung on two pegs driven into the wall. Grabbing a box of cartridges from a nearby shelf, Dibley started cramming bullets through the rifle's loading port as he positioned himself beside the window.

Dole urged his horse into a gallop when he saw the boy run inside. 'They've seen us. Get around the house as quick as you can,' he called to his men. 'Watch for shots from the windows.'

The riders split and Barstow opened hostilities by firing a shot through the thin planking that was the kitchen door. Glass shattered as Dibley fired back through the window and the big outlaw's mount reeled under the impact of a bullet. The rider cursed and vaulted from the saddle a split second before the animal collapsed. For such a big man he was light on his feet, but the brief instant taken to regain his balance proved to be his downfall.

Another shot from Dibley hit Barstow and spun him round, toppling him on to the pile of cut wood. He had the presence of mind to roll over the pile and take what shelter he could behind it. Not that it did him any good for, although still unaware of the fact, he was mortally wounded and already out of the fight.

Craig checked his horse long enough to throw a couple of shots through the front window. If it was intended to intimidate the defenders, the idea failed.

Susan Dibley fired from another window and the bullet zoomed past the gunman's ear. If a wind-blown curtain had not interfered with the lady's sighting, Craig would have been a dead man. He knew it and spurred his mount round the corner of the house.

The remaining riders met briefly at what they thought was a blind spot in the defences, but Dibley emerged from the house and fired round the corner of the building. The two quick shots he fired missed their marks but sent the riders scattering and spurring their mounts to find cover or get out of range. They would need to be quick. Tom Dibley had opened fire as they came in view of the window where he had stationed himself. Previous bad experiences had taught the rancher to keep a clear field of fire all around the house. Tom's shooting did no execution but the trio had to gallop their weary horses another 300 yards under fire before taking refuge in a stand of trees.

'Where's Barstow?' Dole asked as he halted his mount.

'He got hit,' Craig replied as he reined in beside him. 'They got both him and his horse. He looked like he was hit real bad.'

'Maybe he was only wounded.' Dole knew he was being unrealistic even as he said it. Barstow had been his right-hand man and he had placed great reliance on his ability to cope with predicaments like the one they were currently experiencing.

'I'm guessing that he's dead, Mickey. That *hombre* wouldn't have dared come out of the house if he knew that Barstow was still there in shooting condition. Forget about him. Even if he's alive, we can't take a badly wounded man with us.'

Stirling dismounted from his weary horse and peered around a tree-trunk at the ranch house. 'What happens now? I can see horses in a pasture in front of the house but the gate's in easy range for the shooters inside. We're in one hell of a mess. We've lost Barstow, wore out our horses and are likely to get killed trying to steal others.'

Dole growled, 'I'll think of something.' But the tone of his voice indicated that he had no real contingency plan.

It was Craig who came up with a possible solution.

He pointed at the horses grazing in the distance. 'The back of that pasture is out of accurate range for a Winchester. We can break down the fence at the back, get in and take fresh horses.'

'You're forgetting that the sonofabitch in the house is likely to come out shooting,' Stirling told him.

Craig gave a small tight, smile. He had not forgotten. 'From here we can still hit the house and with luck, hit anyone fool enough to show himself. The bullets will carry that far easily with the right amount of elevation. If one man stays here and keeps dropping shots on to the house, the folks there will stay inside. The other two can do a wide detour behind those trees, bust down the back fence and get us some new horses. Pick ones with shoes or nail holes in their feet that show they've been working. We don't want to be bronc-busting at a time like this. Once we have our riding-ponies the rest can be let go. Send 'em hell, west and crooked, so there'll be no fresh horses for any posse to chase us with.'

Dole looked at Craig with a new-found respect. As the newest member of the gang, the latter usually had said little in the past and simply followed along with the others. 'Do you think it will work?'

'I know it will work. That posse hasn't got us yet.'

FOUR

The posse rode to the Harris ranch to pick up pro-
visions, then headed west to cut the trail of the
outlaws. The work was slow and painstaking, the
men riding abreast where the rough country
allowed, scanning the ground and hoping that they
had not missed the tracks because of the big slabs of
rock where they would not show.

As he rode Clem became impatient. Every
minute wasted meant that the killers had extended
their lead. Other riders were feeling the same but
Black appeared to be quite relaxed and whistled
tunelessly as his horse walked easily on a loose rein.

Deputy Weatherby was not sure that he really
wanted to catch up with the outlaws. He had seen a
few examples of their deadly shooting and secretly
doubted that his posse was big enough to keep the
killers running. Dole could reduce their numerical
superiority in one swift ambush.

Black, with his extensive knowledge of outlaw

habits, was gradually assuming the leadership of the posse and Weatherby was looking increasingly unfit for the job. Unconsciously he gave the impression that he preferred not to catch up with Dole and was content to chase him at a safe distance.

Max Hall, one of the posse members from town, was the first to find traces of the fugitives. 'There's tracks over here,' he called to the others.

'Everyone keep back until I get a look at them,' the bounty hunter called.

The others obeyed because while all could see tracks, few could really read the story they told.

Black's experienced eye scrutinized the hoof-prints for a moment. 'It's them,' he announced. 'They're riding hard but their horses are tiring; there are slight drag marks showing on some of the prints.'

'That don't make sense,' said Weatherby. 'They should know better than to run the guts out of their horses.'

Clem disagreed. He had seen Indian raiders use the same tactics. 'They're trying to run us off our feet. You can bet your boots they'll steal fresh horses at the next ranch they come to and run the guts out of them too. We won't be able to replace worn-out horses so easily.'

'That's right,' Black said in support. 'Let's use our heads and try to anticipate where they're going?' He looked at those about him and said, 'I'm a stranger around here. Who knows where the closest ranch is?'

Bill Lyons and Casey Hopkins, the two hands from the Harris ranch, knew the area well and had worked there on round-ups.

Lyons, the younger of the two was a short, heavily built man. He answered first. 'Gus Dibley has a little spread about ten miles up that creek you can see there on your left. The canyon twists all over the place but that's the way a stranger would go.'

Black asked sharply. 'Do you mean there's a shorter way?'

Hopkins an older, wizened man, answered first. 'There is but it's a pretty hairy sort of trail. Injuns used it for ages. Bill and I have been over it a time or two but we never enjoyed the experience.'

'How much time will it save?'

Hopkins looked at Lyons. 'What do you reckon, Bill?'

'About an hour or so,' the younger man replied.

Weatherby sensed that the short cut would be dangerous. 'Is this new trail worth the risk? Dole and the others could be resting just around the next bend in the canyon. What if they double back?'

'What if they murder the Dibley people while we crawl along?' Black was impatient to be in pursuit again. 'I'm taking the short cut and I want one of you cowhands with me.'

'We'll both go,' Hopkins said. Lyons nodded in agreement.

'Count me in too,' Clem said.

Black twisted in his saddle and a grim smile showed as he told the deputy, 'There's four of us going the short way. You can follow the main trail if you like but if Dole sets an ambush or even turns back you'll be in a hell of a fix.'

Weatherby's face flushed with anger. 'I'm the law here and I say who does what.'

'You're right,' Black agreed. Then he added, 'With legally sworn deputies. You didn't swear me in and I know that none of these cowhands was sworn in either. You can take your deputies, if you had the legal power to swear them in, and waste your time and theirs by trailing at a snail's pace and never catching up, but the rest of us are here to do a job. We want to get it over as soon as possible.'

Weatherby saw that the argument was lost. 'I ain't all that sure I had the legal power to deputize anyone,' he admitted. 'So I guess I'll go along with the idea. It's not real smart to split our forces.'

They started again and Lyons took the lead. A few minutes later he turned his mount from the main trail and into what looked like a mass of pine and cedar. The riders ducked under some branches and brushed away others, pulling their hats lower over their eyes as protection against twigs and low branches. More than one rider bumped a foot or a knee against a tree-trunk and Weatherby swore when his horse took him under a low branch and, despite his bending low, its spiky twigs still scraped painfully along his spine. A few uncomfortable minutes seemed to pass like hours before Lyons announced, 'Here it is. We're right where the trail comes out. Just follow me now. At first it will just be steep but there's a razorback ridge we have to cross that can be a bit tricky. Remember – there's no turning around on this trail. It's too narrow. Once we start there's no turning back.'

Con Brady, one of the town posse men, who had more public spirit than riding ability, had been having trouble with the cow pony he had been given at the Ansons'. He glanced at the canyon wall above him and asked, 'What if my horse gives trouble up there?'

'He won't,' Clem assured him.

'Why not?'

'Because he'll be too damn scared. Put a horse in a really bad situation and he gets too scared to give trouble. A real crazy one might do something bad and fall over but I know that one and he ain't suicidal. Just leave his head alone and keep him moving. He'll follow the horse in front.'

Lyons rode across to Brady. 'You're lucky,' he said. 'That iron-grey horse you're on is part mountain goat. On round-ups I've seen Bert Anson ride it in places where a sane man wouldn't ride at all. You probably have the safest horse here.'

Brady looked happier. 'It's about time my luck changed.'

Unobserved by the townsman, Lyons winked at Clem. The story was a fabrication but it gave the rider sufficient confidence in his mount to stop him trying to take over when the horse was best left to figure its own moves.

They went in single file. At first the slope of the trail was not too bad, but the footing was made hazardous by a mat of pine needles and loose gravel that slipped away in miniature avalanches as the horses disturbed it. The riders leaned forward, standing in their stirrups and holding saddle horns while their mounts varied the pace according to the ground. Some slopes could be walked up but there were short, steep pinches where the horse had to plunge forward driven by powerful thrusts of the hindquarters.

They emerged from the timber on to a small hilltop just above the tree line. Here they rested the horses for a few minutes.

Black was impatient with the delay but Hopkins told him, 'Let the horses have a rest. This is the last place that it's safe to stop. From now on the going gets hard.'

'Do you call that easy?' Hall challenged.

The cowhand pointed to a narrow ridge ahead. 'It's easy compared to that razorback ridge we have to go up.'

The ridge lay at right angles to their present position for a couple of hundred yards to where it joined the canyon wall. It was narrow, only a few feet wide with high, almost vertical drops on each side. Halfway along its length there appeared to be a step about two feet high.

Lyons explained. 'It ain't so bad coming down but on the way up, like we're going, a lot of horses dislike that step. You can't let them stop. Some will climb it, some will jump it but it's a long way to the bottom on either side and you can't turn back, so be careful.'

When the horses were rested they started across the razorback. Lyons led the way, then came Weatherby with his deputies, pale-faced and clinging to their saddle horns. Black followed and even he seemed to have lost the cool demeanour he had maintained up till then. Hopkins came after him but Clem waited. It was best not to have too many riders in such a dangerous place at one time.

With varying degrees of confidence horses and riders climbed the precarious path. The spot where the horses had to jump to the higher level caused a degree of anxiety among the townsmen, who had never learned to trust a good horse, but one by one they negotiated the most frightening section of the trail.

'Keep moving,' Lyons yelled. 'Don't bunch up watching the others come across or there'll be no room for them.'

When the way was clear Clem touched the mane of his blaze-faced sorrel. With the confidence of a man who knows he is on a good horse, he urged his mount forward and said quietly, 'Now Rusty. Show them what a good horse can do.'

When all were across the razorback it was a steep climb to the top. When they reached it the riders could see for miles. The main canyon twisted below them, its high red-rock walls rising far above the trees that seemed to fill the valley. But the watchers knew that a view from that angle was deceptive and there were plenty of wide, grassy meadows hidden by the tall trees.

Black frowned when he saw the number of side canyons that fed into the main one. An army could search for a month and still not find a man hidden in that maze.

Lyons pointed to a distant plume of smoke rising from the dark-green pine trees in the valley below. 'That smoke's from the Dibley place.'

'At least it's coming from the chimney and not a burning house,' Weatherby said hopefully.

'Dole and the others didn't burn the Anson house,' Black reminded him. 'They could still be down there.'

FIVE

Craig squinted along the barrel of his Winchester, sighting on the window of the Dibley house. It had taken a few shots to get the right elevation but he knew that more by good luck than good management, at least one bullet had gone through the opening. It had sparked a flurry of shots in return. Most fell short because the defenders had a less well-defined target. A man concealed by shadows and long grass was impossible to see and stood little risk of being hit with a Winchester at nearly 400 yards.

From his vantage point the outlaw saw no puffs of powder smoke from the side of the house facing the horse pasture, so he assumed that his comrades had not been discovered. His fire had attracted all the defenders' attention.

Carefully Craig spaced his shots, fearful of depleting his stock of rifle ammunition too quickly. He had a dozen rounds left when it occurred to him

41

that Dole and Stirling were long overdue. Curious as to what had caused the delay, he crawled back among the trees, then hurried to where he could see the others. He was just in time to glimpse the tiny figures of his former associates disappearing round a bend in the canyon. They had deserted him.

His dark, unshaven face twisted momentarily in anger and he cursed the fleeing pair, but then his rage was gone. Secretly he had expected some sort of treachery as he had been the newest member of the gang and had not been as close as the others.

His own tired horse was hitched in the brush where he had left it. A cold smile briefly crossed his face as he saw the animal. It was nearly exhausted but would do for what he had in mind. Looking towards the end of the canyon where the others had disappeared, he said aloud, 'You think you've got rid of me, Mickey, but I'll have the last laugh yet.'

The posse reached the Dibley ranch about an hour after the attackers left. A dead horse by the wood-pile and a dead man behind it were notice enough that a battle had taken place, but the sight of Dibley himself standing on the veranda with a rifle told them that the defence had been successful.

'I'm George Weatherby, with a posse from Jackson's Creek,' the deputy announced. 'What's happened?'

'We can all see what's happened,' Black said

impatiently. Addressing the rancher he demanded, 'How long since they were here?'

Dibley was a man who liked to do things at his own pace. He ignored the bounty hunter and told Weatherby, 'There was four of 'em but luckily we saw 'em coming. They started shooting first. I shot one *hombre*'s horse and he seemed a bit peeved about it so I shot him too. He crawled over behind the wood pile before he cashed in his chips.'

'Are any of your people hurt?'

'No. They busted some window glass that will be hard to replace out here and they stole some of our horses. I don't know how many but we ain't hurt. By my reckoning there should be three of them coyotes left.'

While the lawman was talking to Dibley, Black and Clem dismounted and walked over to the wood pile.

'This is, or was, an Anson horse.' Clem pointed to the brand on the shoulder. 'There's another three still missing.'

Black growled, 'I don't give two hoots in hell about stolen horses. I want those scum that murdered their owners. That was the most cold-blooded thing I ever saw.'

'Well, one of them won't be killing anyone else. Do you know who he is?'

'From the description, that's Lew Barstow. When Weatherby gets through playing the big lawman, he'll come over and positively identify him.

43

Meanwhile the others get further away for every minute he delays.'

The bounty hunter's mood was not improved when the deputy accepted Mrs Dibley's offer of refreshments before continuing the hunt. At another time he might have enjoyed coffee and cake but now he begrudged every second lost while Weatherby asked irrelevant questions of the family.

The deputy, however, was not completely wasting his time. The two posse men he had brought from town had lost all enthusiasm, so he arranged for them to wait at the Dibleys. They would bury Barstow somewhere suitable, drag away the dead horse and help guard the ranch in case the outlaws doubled back.

While the deputy was finalizing arrangements, Black rode out and scouted around. He had no trouble picking up the trail of three horses but knew that following it would be difficult. It led into a maze of canyons with patches of heavy brush on the floor, pine and cedar on the slopes and towering red cliffs that formed the walls. As the sun sank lower many of these canyons were in deep shadow.

Dole and the others would be hard to find, but Dibley predicted that, being strangers, they would tire themselves riding up blind canyons before they found the one southern exit from the area. 'They'll be hard to find,' he said, 'but there's a ninety per cent chance that they won't find the way out of those canyons. My cattle and the wild game have made a lot of little trails in the brush but most only lead to grass and water.' Then the rancher added what Weatherby did not want to hear. 'You could easily be ambushed in there, so be careful.'

SIX

Craig followed the tracks of his late companions' horses until he found what he wanted: a large expanse of broken, stony ground where tracks would be indistinct. He dismounted and unsaddled his horse. Keeping on rock to avoid leaving foot-prints, he carried the saddle and its fittings into the brush and hid it under a rocky overhang. Then he took the saddle-bags, the blanket and the slicker he had taken from Anson's. When all this was com-bined with the carbine, he had a fair load to carry but he did not intend to carry it far. It took him a while to find the place that suited but eventually he found it at the top of the slope where the canyon walls became almost vertical. There was a shallow cave at the base of the cliff that afforded a good view of the trail. However, the tops of the trees and a thin screen of small cedars concealed the cave from anyone in the valley below. Close by a small trickle of water was dribbling down from the heights.

Craig had spent a large part of his life as a hunted man and had learned more than his share of survival tricks. Unlike most Western horsemen, he had flat heels on his boots and could walk long distances without becoming sore-footed. While his comrades had been looking for valuables at the Anson ranch, he had raided the larder, filling a pair of stolen saddle-bags with cans of beans, tinned sardines, bacon, dried apples and some freshly baked biscuits. To this haul he had added salt, matches, a tin cup and a half-full bottle of whiskey. Without leaving his lair and by rationing his food, Craig could survive for at least a week. He would be hungry and uncomfortable but, if all went to plan, he would remain hidden until the hunters had moved out of the area. Now he only had to wait.

Remembering Dibley's warning, the posse rode carefully, alert for any sign of danger. Black was by far the best tracker and he followed the few prints that showed, while Weatherby checked their progress on a hand-drawn map that the rancher had sketched for them. The map was not drawn to scale and was not as clear as it might have been, but it was better than nothing.

At irregular intervals Black was able to discern the hoofprints of three horses. He said to Clem, 'The same horse has been at the back all along. It seems mighty weary and I reckon it's one of those taken from the Anson ranch. I don't know why that rider didn't get a fresh horse from the Dibleys.'

'Could he be hanging back a bit to see how close behind we are? I've known Indians to use that trick.'

Black did not agree. He glanced at the tall trees and canyon walls. 'Their rear guard would not be able to see far enough. That trick would not work in country like this. From what I've heard, Dole is a ruthless sonofabitch with no loyalty to his men. Anyone who drops behind gets left. And that's why the same horse is lagging behind.'

They reached a fork where they were unsure which canyon to follow and the posse halted while Black and Weatherby tried to relate their location to the map.

Clem rode over to the two cowboys from the Harris ranch. 'Have you ever rounded up cattle in this country?'

Hopkins shook his head. 'No. Only Dibley's cattle are around here. We leave all these canyons to him. The round-ups always started north of his house, where a few of his cattle might have been mixed in with open range stock, but not the other way around. Given the lie of the land, it was easy for Dibley to turn back any other stock that strayed in this direction.'

Lyons volunteered, 'There is a way out to the south of these canyons if you pick the right one. If Dole and the others find it they'll get a long start on us.'

'If that's the case,' Clem said, 'the tracks will lead

into the left fork. I saw that when Dibley was drawing the map. That little creek running out of the right canyon is flowing north. It don't look it from here, but according to what Dibley told us, the one on the right is a long box canyon.'

'There's tracks over here,' Black called. He studied the rocky ground briefly and turned his horse into the canyon on the right.

'If they turned up there, we've got 'em,' Lyons said.

Weatherby looked nervously at their intended path. 'I don't like this. We could run into them on their way back or they could even be watching us now and setting up an ambush. Whichever side sees the other first has the best chance of getting out alive.'

For once, Black agreed with the deputy. 'Let's work forward to that place ahead where the canyon narrows. Then we set up an ambush and catch them as they come out.'

'I sure hope they ain't got the same idea,' Clem observed as he drew his borrowed carbine. A fired shell had been left in the breech as a safety measure. One movement of the lever flicked it out and fed a live round into the firing chamber. Then he fed another bullet through the loading port and was ready to follow Black who had already started riding up the canyon. *He's sure keen to catch up with Dole,* he said to himself.

*

From his shelter Craig saw the horsemen on the trail below. They were too far away to distinguish individual features, but there was something familiar about the rider on the tall, bay horse. The black hat and the hunched-forward seat in the saddle reminded him of someone he had seen before. Then he remembered: Vern Black. What had brought the bounty hunter after the Dole gang? As far as he knew there were no rewards on offer for them, unless the citizens from Jackson's Creek might have decided to offer one. If they had Black must have been near by to be on the scene so quickly.

He was tempted to take a shot at the hated bounty hunter and risk the consequences, but when he looked through the rifle sights his target was too far away. Craig guessed that he might have been able to hit his man but a shot that missed or did not kill would only exacerbate the problem. Lowering the rifle, he glared at the distant rider. 'I'll get you in my sights one day,' he mumbled to himself.

Clem was far from happy as they cautiously approached the narrow section of the canyon. It was the ideal place to set an ambush and there was every chance that Dole would do so just to get the hunters off his trail.

Weatherby was also ill at ease. He felt that the posse was too small and a couple of well-placed shots would soon cancel any numerical superiority.

He slowed his horse and let Black get further ahead. If the bounty hunter wanted to be the first man shot, that was fine by the deputy.

The canyon was barely a hundred yards wide at the point Black selected. The little creek and game trail ran parallel courses down its centre with boulders and dense brush on both sides. After that point the canyon widened out again and slightly changed direction allowing a fairly long view but a twist in its course obscured the sheer cliffs that, according to Dibley, sealed the other end.

Dole and Stirling had already found out about the cliffs. They gazed up at the sheer walls, hoping to find some means of escape even if they had to abandon their horses, but saw none.

After a few sulphurous expletives Dole growled, 'We have to go back and try that other canyon.'

Reluctantly Stirling agreed with him. 'I hope we don't have a posse too close on our heels,' he added.

'Let's stick close to the brush and work our way back slowly. That posse probably don't know any more about this country than we do. Anyone on our trail won't expect us to be coming back. If we're real careful we'll see them before they see us. We'll just hide in the brush till they go past.'

'It sounds nice and simple the way you put it, Mickey.'

'Do you have a better idea?'

51

'What if we ride back there as quick as we can and get clear of this canyon before the posse arrives? Don't forget that Craig's back there somewhere. We haven't heard any shooting but maybe he's keeping the posse busy.'

Dole frowned and shook his head. 'It's too risky. We could run right into them. If we pussyfoot back and have a good look before we cross any open spaces we'll see any posse before they see us.'

The floor of the canyon opened out into a grassy meadow, but the two fugitives stayed in the deep shadow and brush that grew on the western side. Progress would be slow, but they had a better chance of remaining undetected.

The shadow of the rocky walls was creeping across the meadow when a distant movement caught Dole's eye. Turning his mount into the shelter of a pine thicket, he whispered to Stirling and pointed. 'There's a horse over there, feeding in that long grass. Can you see it?'

'I can see it. That's the horse Craig was riding.'

'Are you sure? It could be a mustang. At this distance one bay horse looks much like another.'

Stirling was adamant. 'That's the one Craig was riding. Wait till it turns its head and you'll see a strange sort of broken blaze on its face.'

'You're right. The sweat marks from the saddle are still on it. But if Craig's here somewhere, why has he turned loose his horse?'

'Damned if I know. Maybe he found another one.

He's taken his saddle and bridle. This horse was probably turned loose and just followed up the creek looking for grass and water.'

'It's also left another lot of tracks that should make it easier for a posse to see where we went. The sooner we get out of this canyon, the better I'll like it. We'll keep to the brush and just make our way slowly and quietly.'

Stirling looked across at the grazing horse and, with a note of optimism, remarked. 'If Craig's gone somewhere else on another horse, there's a chance that the posse might see his tracks and follow him.'

Dole remained unconvinced. 'That could happen but the odds against it are pretty long. I wouldn't bet my life on it. The canyon narrows again soon and if anyone knows about this one being a dead end, I reckon we'll find a reception committee waiting there.'

'If they are I hope they have some grub with them. We didn't take much time to eat when we first got away. I'm starving.'

'Starvation's a slow way to die. Lead poisoning is a hell of a lot quicker. Just shut up for a while and follow me. As soon as we can find a good place to hide the horses, I'm gonna creep up to that bottleneck ahead and make sure we don't run into something nasty.'

SEVEN

The ambush that covered the trail was set on both sides of the creek. Clem did not like the location because of the possibility of one side accidentally firing into the other. He voiced his concern to Weatherby but by then the deputy had given up the little control he had. Black was now running the posse.

He looked around, then said, 'I know this ain't the best place, so we'll need to be careful. No one shoots until I do.'

The men took up their positions. Weatherby and Clem positioned themselves on the left side while Black and the two other cowhands settled among the brush and rocks on the right side. They had secured their horses a hundred yards to the rear so that any restless stamping would not be heard by those approaching.

Then the waiting game commenced.

*

Dole and Stirling found a safe place to conceal their horses and the former crept to where he had a view of the pass ahead. He returned a short while later and said quietly, 'There's plenty of cover for me to sneak up there and have a look around, but the trouble is, there could be a dozen men waiting and I might not see them.'

Stirling was not the patient type and argued for simply riding down the trail and taking their chances. 'If they've got us sealed off in here, we're as good as dead anyway, so there's nothing to lose by trying to shoot our way out. There's always the chance too that the posse hasn't got this far yet.'

'What if that rancher has followed us up? He might have got some help from somewhere. He knows this country. We don't. Just wait back here with the horses. I'm going up there to have a look around. If you see me stand up and wave my hat, get the horses up to me pronto and we can make a run for it.'

Following long hours in the saddle the enforced idleness of waiting was creating a lethargic effect on Weatherby and his men. After half an hour intently studying the scene before them the edge was going off the posse's alertness.

A couple of times Clem found himself nodding off. He deliberately moved into an uncomfortable position in an attempt to remain observant. That worked to a degree but then he developed a cramp in his leg and was forced to abandon that idea.

He was tempted to try scouting a little ahead, but he was too far from Black's group to let them know. Because of the chance of being shot mistakenly on the way back, he abandoned that notion. Several times he saw Weatherby start reaching into his pockets for his cigarette makings but each time the deputy remembered where he was and moved his hand back to the rifle he was holding.

Clem was not sure how long he had been waiting when he saw the tops of some bushes moving on Black's side of the creek, about fifty yards from where the hunters were waiting. The manhunter was the only one across the creek that Clem could see but he was too far away to call to him without betraying the trap. Likewise frantic silent signalling might also catch the eye of the person approaching.

Clem picked up a small rock and tossed it on to Weatherby, who was lying near by and appeared to be dozing.

The deputy awoke with a start, snorted and looked around. Still half-asleep, he muttered, 'What's up?' He also raised himself to a sitting position before looking across at Clem, ignoring the finger that the latter placed to his lips, and repeating his question.

The slight sound and sudden movement both caught Dole's attention as he surveyed the scene through a thin screen of bushes. He caught a glimpse of a hat before its wearer ducked down again. He had located one man on the right side of the creek but he himself remained undiscovered. Now he would wait for the next of his enemies to become careless.

Half a mile away Craig sprawled on a rocky ledge and looked down into the valley. He could see the distant horses that the posse had left, each secured by a neck rope to a stout tree. The riders were taking no chances that the animals would break their bridles when the shooting started.

The temptation was strong. It would be simple to steal one horse and let the others loose but Craig decided to stick to his original plan. He would let the posse catch up with Dole. The outlaw had lost the little allegiance Craig might have felt towards him by deserting him. The hunters would be sure that he was far away and would not linger in the area once Dole was apprehended. It meant another couple of days made miserable by discomfort and semi-starvation but it was a big improvement on being dead.

A cold north wind was starting to blow and black clouds were racing across the sky. The night promised to be dark and stormy. He smiled as he thought how uncomfortable the posse would be as they waited in the rain. He would be sheltered in his hideout and had even gathered some dry firewood, though he dared not light a fire while the posse remained in the area. Even if the trees hid the fire's glow, the smell of smoke might betray him. It would be an uncomfortable night wrapped in a sweaty saddle blanket and a slicker, but it was still a night spent in freedom.

'They're waiting,' Dole told Stirling when he rejoined him, 'on both sides of the creek. I saw a hat on the right side and I heard a cough from the brush on the left.'

Stirling swore long and hard, although he was careful to keep his voice down. Then, when he had seemingly exhausted his supply of obscenities, he asked, 'What do we do now?'

Dole pointed to the black clouds rolling across the sky. 'We have the weather on our side. Those sonsabitches ain't got us yet.'

It was dusk when Weatherby crawled across to Clem. 'I'll keep watch here if you want to go and get our slickers off our saddles.'

The same idea had occurred to Clem and he slipped away before the deputy reverted to his usual indecisive state and changed his mind. When he reached the horses he removed the slickers that each man had fastened behind the saddle cantle. Then, as an afterthought, he removed all saddles and carried them to a sheltered place among the rocks. The night promised to be bad enough without the misery of climbing into cold, wet saddles on the following day.

He donned his own coat and made sure he knew which one was Weatherby's, then he bundled up the others and went back up Black's side of the creek. He had not gone far when he met Bill Lyons, who had gone back to the horses on a similar mission. Passing him the three slickers, Clem said softly, 'I reckon you'll need these. I've taken the saddles off the horses and they are out of the weather under some leaning rocks against the canyon wall.'

'That's saved me a lot of trouble. Do you reckon they're still here and likely to come tonight? It will be one hell of a night if they ain't even here.'

'They're here and what's more, I think they know we're here. I'm pretty sure they were spying us out about an hour ago. I don't know when they'll make a break but I reckon they'll try to shoot their way through.'

Lyons laughed softly. 'If that happens I'm glad that I am near Vern Black. He's reckoned to be pretty good with a gun. Your partner Weatherby ain't much of a shot. Folks around here reckon he couldn't hit his finger if it was shoved down the gun barrel.'

Conscious of the darkness that surrounded them, Clem said, 'In this light there'll be no good shots. There'll be some lucky ones and some unlucky ones, depending on who gets hit by what. And try not to shoot across the canyon. If Dole and the others get between us we could shoot each other. Try to get them while they are out in front of us.

59

Weatherby and I are in a bad position if anyone on your side starts shooting sideways.'

The timing was good and Clem returned with his companion's coat just as the rumbling thunder came closer and the first heavy drops began to fall. Then a jagged streak of lightning split the sky above the canyon. It gave little comfort to the men waiting in ambush, making them suddenly aware of the metal weapons in their hands. Lightning was a greater menace than Mickey Dole.

The rain became heavier, falling in torrents on those crouched below as if it was being poured from some gigantic bucket. It beat against their slickers and hats, chilling hands and faces as well as further reducing the range of vision. Hail started bouncing off the rocks and small branches were torn from trees. Within a few minutes the small creek, shining silver in the darkness, became a rushing, roaring torrent that added to the noise of wind-whipped branches and almost continuous thunder. It also created a barrier between the two parts of the posse. Clem could see the others when the lightning flashed, making the yellow slickers show up against the dark rocks and trees. To his dismay he realised that if the outlaws were watching they might have already gained some idea of the ambush positions.

Another flash and an almost instantaneous crack of thunder announced that the storm was directly overhead. After hours of continual watching Clem had a good idea of what was in front of him, then another flash showed two dark shapes that he could not recall seeing before. Then it was dark again. He peered into the darkness and saw nothing. The sound of the creek and the wind and rain meant that the other night sounds were drowned out. If Dole was making a move this would be the time for it.

Clem looked to his right hoping that Weatherby would spot any movement in front of them.

The lightning flashed again and this time he saw two figures barely twenty yards away, moving down the far bank of the flooded stream. While the posse was listening for the sound of horses the pair on foot had moved almost undetected into the centre of the ambush.

EIGHT

'The creek!' Clem yelled. He threw his rifle to his shoulder and directed a stream of lead down into the hollow as fast as he could fire and reload his weapon.

Red muzzle-flashes stabbed the darkness from Black's position and more than one shot whined off the rocks on Clem's side of the stream as the men opposite started throwing lead. Because of limited visibility most shots went high and a few ricocheted off the rocks that sheltered him and the deputy.

Weatherby somewhat belatedly joined in the shooting but, like the others, was mostly firing blind.

Then one of the men in the middle of the leaden maelstrom fired back and five rifles, guided by the gun flash, sent bullets in reply. Another lightning flash briefly showed one man down on the creek bank and another crouching near by. It was not known if the crouching man was hit or was simply

62

taking cover, but the one stretched full length on the ground was certainly out of the fight.

The next lightning flash showed that the crouching man was making a run to escape the trap. A torrent of lead followed him. The man's gun blazed as he halted and returned fire at his tormentors. It proved to be a fatal error. Nobody knew where the shots went, for he too was only firing at stabs of flame in the darkness, but the muzzle flashes gave the posse an approximate aiming point.

When the lightning flashed again two forms with about thirty yards between them were stretched on the sodden ground.

Clem shouted above the racket, 'They're down. Stop shooting.'

Black's voice came back. 'There's another one there yet. Be careful.'

The 'other one' was safely concealed nearly half a mile from where the one-sided battle was occurring. He knew by the intensity of the fire that his former acquaintances had not made a clean getaway. But that did not worry him because his friendship with Dole and the others had only been a matter of convenience. By deserting him they had cancelled out any obligation for Craig to come to their aid.

'Serves you right, Dole,' he chuckled to himself. 'I wonder how smart you feel now?'

But Dole was past feeling anything. When the lightning flashes revealed the two dead men on the ground, Black cautiously led his men down to check their identities. By this time the storm was moving away.

With his hat shielding a lighted match, Black identified the first body. It was Mickey Dole. Before he was forced to drop the match the bounty hunter could see that the outlaw had been hit by several bullets. Once he had identified the man Black hurried to the one further along the trail. He lit another match, recognized the corpse of Stirling, and swore. Angrily he turned to Casey Hopkins and shouted, 'Where's Craig? There were three of these men. Where is the other sonofabitch?'

The older cowhand had been far from impressed by Black's arrogant manner and deliberately took his time in answering. At last he said, 'How in the hell would I know? But look on the bright side, two out of three ain't all that bad.'

'Actually it's three out of four,' Lyons corrected. But the more favourable figures did little to appease Black's anger.

Clem and Weatherby found a place to cross the flooded creek and they joined the others. The former told Hopkins, 'It was lucky that lightning showed this pair when it did. They damn near got past us. Looks like they left their horses and proba-bly hoped to steal ours if they got through without being noticed.'

'We can't stand around here talking,' Black barked. 'Jack Craig's still out there somewhere.

There'll be plenty of time for talking after we catch up with him. He could have got through already.'

Clem had to admit that this was a possibility. He volunteered to go back and guard the horses until morning.

For what seemed to be the first time that night Black nodded in approval at someone else's suggestion. 'Do that,' he ordered. 'The rest of us will keep a watch on the canyon mouth till it gets light. I want that murdering skunk and I mean to have him.'

The next day they searched the box canyon but found nothing except three abandoned horses and two sets of saddlery. The latter discovery only created more uncertainty. The rain had also wiped out any footprints on patches of soft ground, so tracks had become meaningless.

Weatherby was anxious to abandon the search and to get back to the comfort of Jackson's Creek, while Black argued for remaining in the area.

'Don't forget this Craig coyote helped murder the Ansons and could have that money that was stolen from them. We know the other three didn't have it. I reckon he's around here somewhere.'

'You're welcome to stay here,' Weatherby growled, 'but I'm taking these two bodies back to plant beside Barstow, and then I'm going back to Jackson's Creek. We got the three worst actors and Craig was only a new boy. He won't stay on the loose for long. He'll do something stupid and draw attention to himself. If I was you, I wouldn't waste too much time on Craig because there's no reward for him.'

His face flushed with anger, the manhunter snarled, 'I'm not after any reward. That miserable swine murdered two people in cold blood. I won't rest till all that gang are six feet under. I'll see if I can buy some supplies from the Dibley ranch and I'm staying around for a while. As far as I'm concerned the rest of you can go to hell.'

With the danger passed and a degree of success to show for his efforts, Weatherby resumed his role as leader of the posse. 'I don't care two hoots what you do, Black. This posse's going home.'

Taking the dead outlaws, their horses and stolen saddles, the deputy led his men away from the canyon and headed for Dibley's ranch.

Instead of leading them, Clem and Lyons drove the three horses loose until the animals learned to keep up with the others. One horse belonged to the Anson ranch and the other two were Dibley's. Both of Dibley's had a dead man securely roped across the saddle.

Lyons ranged his mount beside Clem and looked at the rugged country around them. 'I don't like Black's chances of finding Craig all on his lonesome. He seems to want him pretty bad. Weatherby reckons there's no reward for any of these *hombres* and I'm a bit curious as to why a money-hungry buzzard like Black would be wasting his time.'

Clem agreed. 'I think he knows something we

don't.' He paused to turn one of the loose horses back into line and continued, 'It could be that he's after the stolen money. If he catches up with Craig and kills him, who's to know what happened to the money?'

'Do you reckon he'd do that?'

'I don't know for sure, but he's answerable to no one. If he catches Craig alive he might let him buy his freedom for what was stolen from the Ansons. I find it hard to believe Black's only a righteously indignant citizen trying to right a wrong.'

Lyons rolled himself a smoke and as he lit it, he agreed. 'I reckon you could be right, Clem.'

From a hidden vantage point Craig watched them leave. He counted the riders and saw that one was missing. He knew immediately who it would be. Vern Black was not giving up the hunt. The man had been on his trail for a year. Several times Craig thought he had evaded him, but invariably the manhunter picked up the trail again. Craig was resolved to waylay his pursuer sooner or later, on terms of his own choosing, and he sensed that the time for such action might have almost arrived. Once alone Black would be vulnerable to an ambush. One man searching such a large area had a daunting task and the approaches to the outlaw's refuge were all through small patches of open ground that he could keep under surveillance.

After checking his rifle sights and placing the

weapon near by, Craig took a can of sardines from a saddle-bag and opened it. After an uncomfortable cold night, oily fish would not normally have been his choice of breakfasts but it was food and it required no preparation. Glaring at the heavily forested landscape below him, he said in a low voice, 'It don't suit me to kill you yet but if you come this way, Black, I'll make damn sure you won't get any further.'

NINE

The posse stopped at the Dibley ranch overnight. They had spent the afternoon burying the dead outlaws at a place away from the ranch where Barstow had been buried. Then Weatherby started sorting through the property the gang had taken. He recognized Sheriff Gleeson's gun and gunbelt and some of the firearms taken in the original breakout, but the ownership of some other items was uncertain.

Because of his short association with the Anson ranch, Clem could only positively identify his stolen rifle, the horses and one of the saddles, an old slick-fork type that Anson himself had used. Randy would have been more useful in that regard but he was miles away, still straightening out the mess left by the raiders.

The deputy finally decided on a compromise. He would hire a buckboard from the Dibleys to take back the stolen property as far as the Anson place.

There Randy would be able to identify some of the stolen items. Weatherby would take what was left and transfer it to the stolen buckboard which he would then return to Jackson's Creek.

Tom Dibley eagerly volunteered to drive the buckboard but his father vetoed the idea. With one of the gang still loose in the vicinity he wanted his son close by. Another pair of eyes and an extra gun were good insurance until such time as the true situation was known.

Black had asked Clem to arrange for him to buy a little food over the next couple of days while he scoured the canyons for Craig. He was still discussing this with the Dibleys when Weatherby, eager to be home, started the rest of the party down the trail.

'That Mr Weatherby is sure in a hurry to get out of here,' Susan Dibley said.

Clem chuckled. 'I think Weatherby is more at home in town than he is out here.' As he spoke he turned slightly and saw that on a distant canyon wall the morning sun was reflected off something shiny. He pointed. 'Could that be some sort of signal?'

Gus shook his head. 'I doubt it – most likely the sun's shining off a bit of quartz.'

Susan disagreed. 'We've lived here for years, Gus, and we've never seen that before.'

'Maybe we just haven't seen it with the sun just at the right time and the right angle. I've been hunting up there. Ain't no reason for anyone to go there.'

'There could be if someone didn't want to be found,' Clem told him. 'Or maybe Black's in trouble and he's signalling. I think I should take a look. What's the shortest way to get there?'

'To reach that place on a horse, don't follow the trail into the canyon. See that brown streak on the canyon wall over there? Head straight for that. It is a bit of a scramble in places but your horse can get up the slope to the base of the cliffs. The brush doesn't grow right up against the rock, so there's a narrow strip you can follow along the bottom of the wall. You'll have to leave your horse when the ground suddenly gets steeper, but I reckon it would be only a hundred or so yards to where you can see that thing shining.'

Clem swung into the saddle and turned Rusty about. 'It's probably a wild-goose chase but I'll have a look. I can catch up with Weatherby later.'

Black was puzzled. He was a competent tracker and in places the soft ground had left a good record of the night's events after the rain had stopped. It was easy to see where Dole and Stirling had emerged from the box canyon and he saw no tracks up the main canyon. Craig had either escaped by that route before the storm or he was still hiding in the box canyon. Before concluding that his quarry had left the area the manhunter would make a thorough search. But he had no intention of riding into an ambush. He would leave his horse outside the box canyon and reconnoitre the area stealthily and on foot. If Craig thought that all the pursuers had left he might become careless and emerge from hiding.

The plan might have worked except for one thing. The intended prey saw the hunter first.

The fugitive could not believe his luck when he saw Black dismount and conceal his horse in a stand of cottonwoods. Seconds later the bounty hunter emerged on foot with a rifle in the crook of his arm. While still partly screened by the trees, he studied the scene before him for about a minute before moving off to disappear deeper inside the brush in the canyon.

Craig was about 400 yards from where the horse was hidden and an idea quickly formed in his mind. He could steal Black's thoroughbred and ride away, leaving him stranded. Alternatively he could wait near the horse and ambush the hunter as he returned. After some consideration he quickly abandoned the latter idea when he recalled Black's reputation with a gun. A shot that missed or only wounded could have fatal consequences for him. Aware that he would need to move quickly, he jammed his hat on his head, picked up the rifle and made his way down through the pines on the slope. Craig made little pretence at stealth because he knew that his enemy was well out of earshot. He slid and scrambled down the steeper sections of the slope making no effort to hide his tracks.

Clem rode Rusty as far as he could and then left the horse ground-tied at the base of a vertical rock wall. There was still enough space for a man on foot to slip through the brush and clamber over rocks as he moved parallel to the cliff. At a place where water dripped down from the rim rock he saw a bootprint in the mud; the track of a flat-heeled boot. He remembered seeing it before in the yard of the Anson ranch house. The print looked recent and for a moment he feared that Craig might be lying in wait. His approach had not been as stealthy as he would have liked, because of the rough terrain.

Inch by inch he worked his way forward, keeping under as much cover as he could. Then he saw what had been gleaming in the early morning sun. It was the shiny inside of a discarded sardine can. A little past the can he saw a crumpled slicker, a pair of empty saddle-bags, and a saddle blanket. The abundant footprints in the soft areas near by showed that Craig had spent a fair while sheltering under the overhanging rock. The hideout was an excellent vantage point. Looking to his right he could just make out the Dibley ranch buildings and to his left there was a good view up the box canyon. Almost directly in front and below him was the scene of the night ambush. Craig had found himself a box seat for all that had happened.

It was not hard to see where the fugitive had left

his refuge. The tracks led straight down the slope, with broken small branches and heavily disturbed ground leaving a clear trail for any reasonably observant person to follow. He's sure in a hell of a hurry, Clem told himself. He was about to turn back and get his horse when the tiny figure of a distant rider burst from the trees and galloped back towards Dibley's.

Clem was sure that the horse was Black's but the lanky figure perched in too-short stirrups was not the animal's regular rider and the man's floppy black hat could never be mistaken for the man-hunter's expensive grey Stetson. He had heard no shooting but knew that Black would never surren-der his horse unless something had gone horribly wrong.

He hurried back to Rusty, mounted and set the horse straight over the steep slope. They slid down in a shower of loose gravel and broken branches and Clem sat back, letting the horse choose its own pace. It was used to rough country and sensed its rider's urgency. The sorrel would not rush blindly and had no intention of committing suicide. It would speed up where the ground was easy and stop and look where it appeared to be treacherous. At the foot of the slope the creek was much narrower than it had been during the storm and the horse cleared it in one bound. A plunge up the slope on the other side and they reached the trail. It was then that Clem was torn between two possible courses of action. Should he look for Black, in case he was wounded, or should he immediately set out on Craig's trail?

Deciding that he should check on Black's condition first, he backtracked the other horse and turned his mount up the box canyon. Quickly he found where the horse had been tied and prints in the soft earth showed that Craig had approached from the same direction as he had. The bounty hunter was on a wild-goose chase.

Clem drew his Colt and fired a shot into the air. The report echoed around inside the high cliffs. He waited a few minutes and was debating firing another shot when Black emerged from the brush near by panting, red-faced and obviously very angry. 'What in tarnation is all that noise? You've given the game away, you dumb sonofabitch.'

Clem kept his temper intact but derived a great deal of enjoyment from his reply. 'At least this dumb sonofabitch still has a horse.'

'What do you mean?'

'I mean that Craig disappeared with your horse about half an hour ago. You were barking up the wrong tree.'

Black went pale with rage. 'Why didn't you stop him? Why did you let him get away?'

'I was too far away to do anything about it – and I thought you might have been hurt.'

'Give me that horse.'

'Go to hell. It took me a long time to find a horse

like this and I don't intend handing him over for you to ride to death. I'll ride back to Dibley's and see if he can arrange a horse for you but that's all I'll do for you.'

'You're letting a dangerous outlaw escape.'

'You let him escape. Now I suggest you start walking. I'm going to warn the posse that Craig's loose again.'

'You're going nowhere.' The statement was accompanied by the double click of a weapon being cocked.

Clem wheeled his horse to see Black holding his rifle, pistol-fashion, in his right hand. The man-hunter's face was contorted with anger and there was no doubt he meant it when he snarled. 'Get off that horse. I can shoot you and blame it on Craig, so don't do anything stupid.'

'I didn't figure you for a horsethief, but you win.' Clem prepared to dismount.

Black was used to dealing with desperate men but relaxed a little because he expected no trouble from an ordinary cowhand.

Clem made his move as he swung down from the horse. Black would have been wary while he remained in the saddle or after he had dismounted, so his best chance for surprise was in between the two positions. Shortening the near rein preparatory to dismounting, he turned Rusty into the right posi-tion. Then as he swung his right leg over the rump he slammed his foot on to the rifle barrel, forcing

76

the muzzle down. Simultaneously he smashed a backhanded blow to the side of Black's head. The rifle went off, kicking a fountain of gravel under the horse. It snorted and jumped sideways but its rider was already on his feet and launching himself at the bounty hunter.

'I'm gonna kill you,' Black roared.

TEN

Clem did not doubt that his opponent meant what he said and frantically grabbed the Winchester's barrel while hooking a hard left to Black's head. They clinched with the bounty hunter clinging grimly to the rifle as he sought to lever another round into the breech. It was fortunate for Clem that that action took two hands because he still had one hand free and used it to pluck one of Black's guns from its holster. A look of horror came over other's face as he realized he had made a potentially fatal mistake. He had another revolver on his left hip but he knew that he would be dead if he attempted to draw it.

'Drop the rifle or I'll kill you,' Clem ordered. The stolen weapon felt a little awkward in his left hand, but at that range he would not miss.

Black heard the hammer come back to full cock. 'Don't shoot. I'll drop it.' He was as good as his word.

'Step away and get your hands up. Don't think of going for that other gun because you won't make it.'

'You wouldn't shoot me in cold blood.'

'Why not? You were going to murder me and steal my horse. I'm quite within my rights to shoot a horsethief, let alone a murderer.'

'I was only bluffing. That Craig *hombre* is a real murderer, and while we are talking here he's getting away. I have to get after him.'

'The way he's headed, he's likely to run into Weatherby and the others. The back of the gang's broken now. He won't last long and you won't either unless you do what I say.'

'I'm not fool enough to draw against a man who already has the drop on me.'

'Good. Now unbuckle that gunbelt, drop it and step back.'

With no other option, Black reluctantly obeyed.

Carefully Clem picked up Black's rifle and, never taking his eyes off his prisoner, quickly levered another shell into the breech. 'I don't want you shooting me in the back as I ride away. I'll leave this down the trail a bit.' He tossed both of Black's Schofield revolvers into the shallow creek beside the trail. 'You can fish them out after I leave. I'll tell Dibley where you are. He might bring a horse out for you.'

As he mounted his horse Clem heard Black growl. 'Nobody does this to Vern Black. I'm gonna kill you, Shaw.'

'You mean you'll try,' Clem replied as he wheeled Rusty away and touched him lightly with the spurs.

When he advised the Dibleys they were both relieved and concerned. They were relieved that Craig was no longer in the area but were concerned as to how Black would behave when he arrived at the ranch. They had no doubt that he was a dangerous man.

'He'll have cooled down a bit by the time he gets here and I think he'll be happy to pay for any help you give him.'

Tom Dibley had been busy rounding up the horses that Dole had scattered. They had mostly just fed around the break in the fence, so they were soon secured. As he was repairing the break the boy had heard a horseman galloping near by. He told the others, 'I just caught a glimpse of that big racer Black had and thought he was hurrying to catch up with the posse. I didn't know it was Craig.'

'Looks like he's doubled back on his tracks,' Clem said. 'He might run into Weatherby and the others but I'll see if he's left a trail I can follow. You can tell Black where I've gone.'

Following Tom's directions, Clem had no trouble picking up Craig's tracks. The wide-apart prints showed that the outlaw had been riding hard, making no attempt to cover his tracks. At first Craig had ridden on the open ground beside the main trail but then the canyon narrowed at one point and he was forced on to the trail. As the ground had been marked by the posse's mounts, it made tracking difficult. Craig had slackened the pace by then, He knew there were riders ahead of him and had no intention of blundering into them. At a point where the canyon opened out, the thoroughbred's tracks turned off into the brush.

Clem's first reaction was to follow Craig but he knew that Weatherby and the others would not be far ahead; he thought it more prudent to warn them of Craig's presence.

He found the posse quicker than he expected. They had halted along the trail and were letting the horses graze as they waited for him. Weatherby was not looking pleased.

'Where have you been, Shaw? You're holding us up. I was beginning to think that you had struck trouble somewhere.'

'You thought right and there's a lot more trouble around.'

This was not the news that the deputy wanted to hear. 'What do you mean?'

Clem explained what had happened and the others were stunned by his revelation. The close proximity of Craig was something that nobody had considered, and the report of Black's reaction left them shaking their heads in disbelief.

'Are you saying that you have tracked Jack Craig to somewhere near here?' Weatherby asked nervously.

'That's right. His tracks were over in the brush on the right side of the trail. He might have passed you already or he could be lying low, waiting for a chance to slip past you.'

It was Lyons who suggested their next course of action. He said to Clem, 'What if the others stay here to guard the trail and you and I try to pick up his tracks? That way we'll know if he's in front or behind us.'

'You might find out the hard way if that sneaky sonofabitch is over there somewhere waiting with a gun,' Hopkins warned.

'It's the only way we can tell for sure,' Clem said. He turned to Lyons. 'I'll go with you if you still want to have a look.'

'Good. Let's go.'

The pair crossed the open ground and separated slightly when they reached the tangled brush and jumble of boulders beneath the towering cliffs. Many areas were inaccessible to a horse so, despite the hard ground, tracking was not as difficult as the searchers had expected. Hoofprints were few and far between but the muddy sides of overturned stones showed where the horse had passed.

It was not long before they knew that Craig had slipped by the posse but neither man could accurately assess the amount of start that the fugitive had on them.

They rode back and broke the news to Weatherby. Though he pretended to be disappointed, he was secretly pleased. The sooner he got back to patrolling the quiet streets of Jackson's Creek the happier he would be.

ELEVEN

The posse had a few half-hearted tries at picking up the outlaw's trail but it soon became obvious that Craig was an expert at concealing tracks. The deputy was tired of the whole exercise and only too eager to abandon the search. His men had experienced a fair measure of success accounting for three of the four fugitives for no loss of life on their side.

It was late afternoon when they reached the Harris ranch, tired, hungry and dirty. Jud and his wife Clara made them welcome. Maryanne emerged from the kitchen a short while later. She had seen them coming and started preparing food. Clem would have liked to socialize with her but too much was happening and the girl seemed to be coming and going continually as she brought food from the kitchen.

Questions and answers flew back and forth, with Weatherby doing most of the talking. He shrugged off the fact that Craig was still at large after leaving Black afoot.

'He's small fry,' the deputy assured his listeners. 'He won't get far. Some lawman miles from here will eventually pick him up.'

Until then Clem had said little, but he did not agree with Weatherby's assessment of the situation. 'I wouldn't be too sure about that,' he said. 'Craig outfoxed Black, stole his horse, slipped past us and hid his tracks. I reckon he's an old hand at the outlaw game. Black seemed mighty keen to catch up with him even before he stole his horse. I think he knows something that we don't.'

'The Ansons' cattle money is still missing,' Clara said. 'Maryanne and I have been over at their place helping Randy get things fixed up. Their son Harry was over here from Chicago to arrange the funeral. He has inherited the ranch but is thinking of selling it. He had to rush back to Chicago after the funeral, so Randy is running the place.'

'I wonder where that leaves me?' Clem said.

It was Maryanne who answered. 'I heard Harry tell Randy to keep you on until he finally decided what to do. You have a job for a while if you want it. There's too much work there for one man. He might sell the place eventually but that could take time.'

'That's comforting to know. Now my only worry is Vern Black.'

'I think you'll find he was only bluffing,'

Weatherby said. 'He has to stay within the law the same as everyone else.'

Jud Harris was not so sure. 'From what I heard Black's pretty good with a gun and the only laws he stays within are the ones he makes himself.' He looked hard at Weatherby. 'Could you arrest him if he decided to take the law into his own hands?'

'That won't happen,' the deputy said with a confidence that he did not really feel. He knew Black's reputation with a gun and dreaded the thought of getting involved in a shoot-out with him.

'I sure wouldn't like to be that Craig fella.' Harris chuckled. 'He made Black look mighty stupid when he stole his horse. That story will haunt him for the rest of his life. Until he corrals Craig one way or another he's going to be a bit of a joke. I'll take a bet now that he won't bring Craig in alive if he catches up with him.'

'I hope he doesn't take his anger out on Clem,' Maryanne said.

'He can try,' the cowboy said, 'but I'll make him earn his reputation. Gunfighters and barroom brawlers are like bucking horses. Most people are scared because of what they might do and often, when they're tried out, they're not as good as they were claimed to be.'

'Sounds like you're talking from experience,' Harris observed.

'I've been around long enough to know that not all men who act tough really are tough. But I'm not fool enough to underestimate a man I don't know or take any chances I don't have to. I'd much prefer that this incident didn't happen but no man steals my horse while I'm in a position to do something about it. Also, I'm still not sure that he didn't intend to kill me. I wouldn't trust Vern Black as far as I could throw a bull buffalo by the tail.'

Tex Lanham saw himself as a lucky man There were many worse jobs on the Box C ranch than taking supplies up to the Split Rock line shack. At present it was empty but the fall round-up was over and a rider would be stationed there all winter to stop cattle drifting ahead of the freezing north winds. If they passed the shack at Split Rock and were not turned back they could move into dangerous areas where they would starve and freeze to death.

Line riding was a lonely job and Tex was glad that he would not be doing it. In another week he would quit the Box C and live in town on his savings until work started again with the spring round-up. The packhorse he was leading carried the first load of necessities for the line rider. There were few luxuries but the man would be reasonably well supplied. Milton Carr had a fine reputation for looking after his men.

Two miles short of his destination, Tex Lanham struck trouble.

A rider on a lean bay horse appeared from around the spreading branches of a big blue spruce. He had a sawn-off shotgun in one hand and the twin barrels, like a pair of unblinking eyes, were aimed at the Box C rider.

The newcomer was wild-eyed, dirty and bearded. In a rasping voice he ordered, 'Stay right where you are. Make one wrong move and I'll kill you.'

'Hell, I ain't movin',' Tex answered nervously. 'Just be careful that cannon don't go off.'

'What are you doing here?'

'I'm just takin' supplies up to the Split Rock line shack. There'll be a rider up there as soon as it starts gettin' cold.'

'What sort of supplies?'

'Canned goods, coffee, flour, sugar, salt, tobacco, matches, stuff like that. The line rider will bring up another packhorse load when he comes later. He could be up there for months.'

'Any whiskey?'

'Not in this load.'

Craig gestured with the barrels of the shotgun. 'Get off that horse and start unpacking that pack saddle. Do as you're told and you won't get hurt. Get the tobacco out first. I'm dying for a smoke.'

Tex did as he was told. Meanwhile his captor dismounted and hitched his horse to a nearby tree but at no time did he let down his guard. He strolled across to where the contents of the pack panniers were being laid out and selected a can of peaches. He tossed it to the cowhand and ordered him to open it. While Tex was searching among the camp gear for a can opener, Craig helped himself to tobacco and cigarette makings. Then, seating himself on a log, with the shotgun nearby, he lit up the first cigarette he had smoked since the raid on the Jackson's Creek bank. With obvious enjoyment he blew clouds of smoke into the air and even smiled a little as Tex wrestled open the top of the peach can.

The cowhand was still wearing his old cap-and-ball Remington .44 but was not tempted to use it. The loads had been in the cylinder for some time and it had been weeks since the weapon had been fired. He was not even sure that all the caps were still on the nipples. A tight holster high on his right hip made a quick draw impossible. His best chance of survival was to co-operate and hope that Craig would leave when he had stolen all he wanted.

There was something familiar about the gunman and Tex tried to remember where they had met before. He watched his captor who had selected a fork from among the cooking utensils and, having finished his smoke, was spearing peach pieces from the can and devouring them hungrily. Both hands were full but the shotgun was still in easy reach across his lap.

Though he had not intended to draw unfavourable attention to himself, the prisoner looked too hard for too long. Craig suddenly stopped eating, laid aside the peach can and picked up the gun. In a low voice laden with menace, he demanded, 'Why are you staring at me?'

Clearly alarmed, Tex replied, 'I didn't mean to stare. It's just that I thought I might have known you. You remind me of a fella I saw once in Texas.'

It was a fatally wrong answer.

As casually as he would swat a fly, Craig fired one barrel of the gun and his target was close enough to collect all nine heavy buckshot slugs. The impact drove Tex backwards and left him a writhing heap on the ground. His killer calmly picked up the peach can again. He saw no need for another shot and seconds later the fallen man ceased all movement.

'Serve you right for having a good memory,' Craig told the dead man. 'You probably did see me in Texas but I don't want word of that getting around. I'm quite happy for the law around here to be looking for someone named Craig.'

The sun was almost set when Clem prepared to leave the Harris ranch. It would be nice to be back in the bunkhouse after a bath and some clean clothes but for a couple of reasons, he was strangely reluctant to return to the Anson ranch. He had formed a close friendship with Lyons and Hopkins and also enjoyed the brief period with the family. He also tried to fool himself that he had not been badly smitten by Maryanne. But he did not know whether or not he had made any sort of favourable impression on her. She seemed the same with everyone: bright and friendly.

Weatherby would spend the night with the Harris family but Clem was in riding distance of his home base. He would leave the Anson horses and stolen equipment behind for Randy to identify when the deputy brought it to the ranch the next day. He could have brought the horses but hoped they would give him an excuse to see Maryanne again when he went to retrieve them.

It was only a couple of miles cross-country to Anson's but Clem was suddenly tired. In his present state, the final stage of the journey would be a long one. He had thanked the Harrises and was going to collect Rusty from their corral when he heard pounding hoofbeats approaching. The oncoming rider was not sparing his mount and Clem knew who it would be.

TWELVE

Black had been riding hard. The horse he had purchased from Dibley along with an unwanted McClellan saddle had been ridden to exhaustion. Patches of white lather showed on its neck, shoulders and flanks and it was unsteady on its feet. Its sides were heaving when eventually it was hauled to a stop.

The bounty hunter dismounted with only one thought on his mind. 'Where's Shaw?' he demanded.

Clem stepped clear of the small group who had been waiting on the ranch veranda. 'I'm here, Black. Just cool down a bit.'

'Cool down,' Black yelled. 'You're telling me to cool down after you let Craig steal my horse and stopped me from following him? You're going to pay for what you did this morning.'

'I had no way of stopping Craig from getting away. I was too far from the scene but I sure as hell wasn't going to let you treat my horse the way you've treated the one you've just been riding. Craig had too long a start and he'd already slipped past the posse before I could warn them.'

'And I'll bet you told him where the posse was,' Black accused. 'I reckon you and Craig were in cahoots. You helped him escape. Didn't you?'

Trying to keep his temper in check, Clem asked, 'Now why would I do that?'

With a note of triumph in his voice the bounty hunter said, 'Because he paid you off. He had the money taken from the Anson ranch. We didn't find it on the other gang members so Craig must have been carrying it.'

Weatherby could see a bad situation evolving and felt he should at least make a token effort to restore calm. 'That's not necessarily right, Black. Craig was only a minor member of the gang. Chances are Dole stashed it somewhere.'

'When I want the pig I'll rattle the bucket,' Black snarled. 'Till then I'm talking to Shaw – so stay out of this.'

Having made his token effort Weatherby fell into an affronted silence. He could see where this situation was going and wanted no part of it.

'You're barking up the wrong tree,' Clem said. 'But there's something a bit odd about the way you're busting a gut to catch up with Craig. Maybe you're after the money you think he's carrying. So far as we know there's no reward out for him, so I'm a bit puzzled as to why a money-hungry buzzard like you is so keen to catch up with him. What's really going on with you and Craig?'

His voice trembling with rage, Black brought his hands to close proximity to the guns on his hips. 'You're going to answer a few questions, Shaw, or I'm going to shoot you like a mangy dog.'

'You can try any time you like but at this range I'm not so bad a shot that I'll miss you, even if you do get me. If you go for those guns you can count on me getting at least one shot into you. I've seen your type before, Black, and I'm calling your bluff. You can act civilized or start shooting.'

A man less angry might have stopped and thought but Black went for his guns.

The move had not taken Clem by surprise but he was still amazed at the speed with which his opponent's guns cleared leather. A fraction of a second before he could fire his own gun he could see the muzzle of Black's gun aiming at him. He knew that the bounty hunter would get in first shot and could only hope that he survived long enough to fire back.

Vaguely he heard the report of a gun but felt no impact from a bullet. He fired his first shot just as Black's gun roared. In the dim light Clem saw a vivid red flash and to his surprise saw the gun spin from the other's hand. But Black was a two-gun man and already his left-hand gun was coming on to the target.

This time Clem got the first shot away and he saw his adversary stagger backwards, obviously hit but still dangerous.

Black, like many two-gun men, was not ambidextrous and made a determined effort to transfer his gun to his right hand, giving Clem just enough time to aim his next shot. The gun kicked hard against his hand and despite a cloud of powder smoke and poor light he saw his target twisted sideways before slumping in a heap on the ground.

'You got him,' Hopkins yelled.

Amazed that he was still alive and unwounded, Clem approached the fallen man and saw that further caution was unnecessary. Both guns had fallen from Black's hands and he lay unmoving.

Lyons walked across to where the victor stood. 'Did he hit you at all?'

'No. His first shot must have missed. My shot must have hit his gun.'

Weatherby joined them. 'There was something funny about Black's first shot. It made an odd sort of noise and the second shot sounded a bit funny too.'

'I was too busy to notice,' Clem admitted.

Harris picked up Black's right-hand gun. There was a jagged split along several inches of barrel. 'Well I'll be danged. The gun burst.'

'Maybe Clem's shot went straight down the barrel,' Hopkins suggested.

Harris's wife and daughter appeared on the

veranda with a lamp.

'Who was shot?' Maryanne asked anxiously.

Her father answered, 'It was Black. He's dead. You and your mother stay there.' Then as an after-thought he held the gun in his hand closer to the lamp. Through the burned and split barrel he could see one bullet jammed into the base of another. He took the gun over and showed Weatherby. 'Looks like Black's first shot got stuck in the barrel and the second one hit the bullet and busted it open.'

'Now how could that happen?' The deputy looked at the wreck of the Schofield's barrel and shook his head as though in disbelief.

'I think I know,' Clem said as he joined them. 'I threw Black's guns in the creek this morning to stop him shooting me as I rode away. Mostly water doesn't get into metallic cartridges but one must not have been as well sealed as it should have been. The water must have dampened part of the powder charge but it would not affect the priming cap. There was enough power of some kind to push the bullet into the barrel and it stuck there in the rifling. Black's second shot went off like it should and the bullet burst the barrel when it hit the other slug.'

'If that's the case,' Hopkins sounded disap-pointed, 'where did Clem's first shot go?'

'It must have been a clean miss,' Clem admitted sheepishly. 'I was very lucky.'

'You're doubly lucky,' Weatherby said in his most official voice. 'We all saw Black fire the first shots. It was a clear case of self-defence. There won't be any charges coming out of this.'

'That's a relief. What happens now?'

'You might as well head for home. I'll take care of things here,' the deputy said.

'Clem,' Clara Harris called, 'would you like a cup of coffee or something to steady your nerves before you go home?'

'No thanks, Mrs Harris. I'd better get on my way.' He hoped that in the darkness the others would not see how shaken he was.

Craig eventually found the place he sought. It was a shallow cave in the canyon wall, well screened by brush and close to water. With a good supply of stolen food he could live there undetected for more than a week, but there was no feed for the three horses he had now acquired. Most outlaws would be loath to part with their main means of escape but Craig was using a plan that had worked for him several times before. He would lie low close to the scene of the crime while the lawmen searched far and wide for him. They would never expect him to hang around when he had horses at his disposal and the main focus of the hunt would be much further afield. When the search widened he could walk out until he found a suitable horse to steal and would reappear a hundred miles away with a new name. He had not always been Jack Craig. Essentially he was a loner but had joined other gangs at different times when in unfamiliar areas. His was the new face that few people seemed to remember, the minor player who appeared for a while and disappeared before his other associates ran out of luck.

The raid on the Jackson's Creek bank had seemed safe enough because nobody knew that there would be a big crew of paid-up trail hands in town at the time. But his luck was not all bad, a larger, better-organized posse might still have run him to earth. He would be more careful in future.

The final phase of his plan was to turn loose the horses. They would be found and a hunt would start but few men in the cattle country would envisage a fugitive remaining on foot when he had horses at his disposal.

As he watched the horses walk uncertainly away Craig smiled to himself. The plan had always worked before because he always used it in a different locality. As long as he did not become careless, Craig saw no reason that it should fail this time.

THIRTEEN

No lights were showing in the ranch house when Clem dismounted at the Anson place. He unsaddled Rusty, put him in the corral and rubbed his back. After pumping water into the trough he groped his way into the darkened feed shed to the large tin-lined box where oats were stored. He scooped some up in a bucket, he went outside and poured the grain into the manger attached to the fence. Then he went to the bunkhouse and without lighting the lamps felt his way to his bunk. With weariness weighing heavily upon him he removed hat, boots and gunbelt and flopped on to the bunk. He dragged a blanket over himself and quickly fell asleep.

The sun was high the next morning before he presented himself to Randy after a bath and a change of clothes. Randy was busy at Anson's writing desk when Clem came in.

'So you finally woke up,' Randy said with a rare

grin. 'How did the big manhunt go?'

Clem told him all that had happened and had no trouble holding his companion's interest. Occasionally he asked a question but mostly he just listened in silence.

At the end of the narrative Randy asked, 'What about the money? Was any of that recovered?'

'Not a cent. Either it's been hidden somewhere or Craig has it. What's been happening here?'

Randy's mouth twisted into a rueful smile. 'You had all the fun. I've been stuck here until yesterday with my cousin. It's hard to imagine Harry was raised on this ranch because he don't know much about the cattle business or how the place should be run. He's a right royal pain in the rear end.'

'There's a couple of our horses still at the Harris ranch and a saddle or two that might belong here,' Clem said. 'Weatherby will bring the stuff over in a buckboard tomorrow, but I was too dead beat to bring the horses back. They'll travel better after a night's rest too. Do you want me to go over and collect them today?'

Randy thought for a while, then said, 'No – I'll go after I identify the stuff of ours that Weatherby has recovered and he picks up that stolen buckboard and team. I want to find out if Weatherby is going to make another search around here. Jud Harris might know what's being done. I figure I should start doing my bit to avenge my relatives now. Just keep working those horses. I want them to bring a good price when the ranch is sold.'

After breakfast Clem went into the feed shed and filled another bucket with oats. He would give Rusty another feed before turning him out on the grass again. As he emerged he saw Randy standing at the kitchen door frowning.

'You shouldn't be using those oats,' the tall man said.

'I like to keep a bit of hard feed in Rusty in case I need him for a bit of hard riding. With Craig loose somewhere I might need a good horse in a hurry. If a horse is used to oats you can carry some with you and don't lose time looking for grazing.'

'I know that, but those oats belong to the ranch and that horse is your own private one. You should be riding ranch horses.'

'You can take the cost of the oats out of my pay that's coming,' Clem said sharply. He was in no mood for such a trifling argument and added, 'You know, Randy, I've never met your cousin Harry but from what you told me, you seem to be giving a good imitation of him.'

Randy's stern features relaxed into a smile. 'You could be right, Clem. I guess all this responsibility is going to my head. I want to hand this ranch over as a profitable concern and don't want it going to blazes just because of what happened.'

Weatherby arrived later in the morning with Dibley's buckboard and a few items that had been taken from the raid on the Anson ranch. Clem was pleased to find his own rifle and saddle-bags among the stolen equipment but was not so pleased when the deputy said they would have to be held as evidence until future court proceedings were resolved. He would leave Dibley's buckboard and team at the Anson ranch and bring back the banker's wife's vehicle and horses that the gang had originally stolen during their breakout. By arrangement Gus Dibley would collect his buckboard on his next visit to Jackson's Creek for supplies. At that time Weatherby would pay him for the hire of his buckboard and horses.

The men from town did not delay long at Anson's and after the generous hospitality at the Harris ranch they were not keen to try any fare that the pair of bachelors would offer by way of refreshment. Weatherby completed his business with Randy and left soon after.

An hour later the new boss of the Anson ranch had ridden over to see Jud Harris, leaving Clem busy with the fresh horses. He had ridden them all before so the hard work was done. Now it was just a case settling them down with a few longer rides.

He had just mounted a little bay gelding when the animal suddenly pricked its ears and looked sideways. Clem followed his horse's gaze and saw Randy riding hard towards him. The speed of his approach was a sure sign that something was wrong. Puzzled, Clem rode out to meet him.

'There's trouble,' Randy announced as they met.

'I just met Bill Lyons coming over to see us. A rider from the Box C was at Harris's. Something's happened to one of their men. He was taking supplies up to a line cabin. His horses came back to the ranch this morning.'

'Maybe they just got away from him.'

Randy's face looked grim as he said, 'That bay thoroughbred of Black's was tailing along with them – the horse that Craig stole. Milt Carr is raising a posse. I just came home to get a better horse and to collect my rifle and a few things I might need.'

'Do you want me to come with you?'

'No. Stay here and keep a close eye on the horses. Craig might try to steal one.'

'So you think he's on foot?'

'I'm not sure. The horses might have got away from him or he might have picked up another one somewhere. We won't know until we've had a good look around. We have to find out what happened to Carr's man, too. I knew him as Tex but never did know his last name. We'll be using the Box C as our main base. If Craig's still in the area we'll get him, and this time we won't have that jackass Weatherby underfoot.'

Craig had done all that he could to conceal his new hideout and make it comfortable. As part of his plan he had helped himself to more supplies than he ever expected to need. It had taken him several trips to carry his loot from the murder scene to his shelter and he had gone by a different route each time to avoid making a path. Then he carefully brushed out tracks and replaced any stones that he might have accidentally turned over. Damp earth on the bottom of an overturned stone would not be missed by a good tracker and Craig was not one to underestimate his enemies.

He knew that the hunters would come in the next day or so and they would be looking for signs of a killer fleeing the scene. If he had laid the false trail properly they would not be long in the vicinity. Until they left, though, there could be no cooking fires and he would be sick of cold, canned food, but he would be safe. As soon as the posse had left the area he would be able to camp in relative comfort for a few days until it was time to steal another horse. That would present no difficulty. In his early years Craig had lived with the Utes and could steal horses with the best of them. For the present, though, he would lie low and wait. He had found a hidden spot from which he could overlook the place where Tex's body still lay amid the plundered supplies. He knew that it would not be long before someone was sent from the ranch house to investigate the dead man's failure to return. The loose horses would make their way home but would not be in a hurry if the grazing was good. Watching and waiting was monotonous but Craig was working to a well-used plan that so far had never failed him.

The riders arrived about noon, eight of them.

Though a couple of hundred yards away their dismayed voices carried faintly to the hidden listener. He smiled to himself as he saw them riding around the scene. The more they rode over tracks, the less likely they were to discover him.

Milt Carr jumped from his horse and hurried over to where Tex lay. As if to wipe away feelings of shock and sorrow, he brushed a hand over his eyes. He had liked Tex and his man's sudden death momentarily left him stunned.

Jud Harris also dismounted and said gently, 'There ain't much we can do for him now, Milt.'

Carr answered in a voice shaking with anger. 'There is, Jud. We can get the murderin' sonofabitch that did this. Nobody kills a Box C man and gets away with it. I'll get him if it's the last thing I do.'

The others dismounted and Casey Hopkins had no doubts about the killer's identity. 'Craig killed him for sure. You can see where he was hit by a shotgun. Black's shotgun was on his horse when Craig took it.'

Randy had been looking about the scene. 'There's a pack saddle lying over there but no riding saddles. Craig must have got another couple of horses from somewhere. Could there be someone else with him – someone we don't know about?'

Harris had another opinion. 'Supposing he used

the other riding saddle to pack supplies on?' He asked Carr, 'Do you know what was stolen from here?'

The other rancher looked around before replying, 'I sure do because I helped Tex pack it. Looks like half the canned goods are gone along with a side of bacon. Looks like a frying pan and a coffee pot are gone too. There might be some flour, coffee, salt and sugar scattered around in this mess or he might have taken that as well.'

'That's awkward stuff to pack on a riding saddle,' Hopkins said. 'I can't figure out why he didn't take the pack saddle.'

'Maybe he hopes to sell one of the saddles later,' Randy suggested. 'He might be short of cash.'

'Ain't you forgetting that he's probably got all that money he took from the Ansons?' Harris reminded.

'We're only guessing about that,' Randy replied. 'He might never have had it. Dole was the leader of the gang. He might have hid it somewhere.'

'There's another possibility,' Harris said gravely. 'Black accused your man, Shaw of taking a bribe to let Craig go. Do you think Shaw might have it?'

Randy shook his head.' Shaw might not be too bright but I reckon he's honest.'

Hopkins did not agree fully with that assessment. 'Shaw don't say a lot but he's smarter than you think, Randy. He struck me as being honest, though, and I wouldn't put too much faith in anything Vern Black said.'

Harris looked doubtful. 'We all think we know people but some can change when there's a lot of money involved. But let's get Tex's killer first.'

Carr pushed back his hat, scratched his head and looked up at the canyon walls as if he expected to see a message written there. At last he asked, 'Where do we go from here?'

A few minutes of argument followed before agreement was reached. A rider would be sent back for a wagon to take Tex's body to town. Carr would sort through the abandoned supplies in an attempt to discover what was missing while the others scouted the area looking for Craig's trail.

'Looks like he's fitted himself out for travelling,' Harris said. 'I reckon he'd be making for Canada round about now.'

Hopkins was not so sure. 'I can't help wondering where he got those other two horses from.'

'Could be that someone brought them to him,' Randy suggested.

Harris interjected. 'How would his partner know where to come?'

Carr cut short any further discussion. 'I've got work to do here. I suggest that you boys ride around and try to find out which way our man, or men, went.'

FOURTEEN

A week passed with no sign of Craig. The posse had searched all the trails leading out of the area but found nothing. In the end they dispersed, after agreeing that their man was long gone.

Randy had gone to see a lawyer in Jackson's Creek, having said that he would be away for a couple of days. Clem continued working the horses. All had settled down so he was now increasing the length of the rides and testing their previous experience with stock. He would ride up to small bunches of cattle, head them off if they attempted to flee, and check them over. They were running on open range and there was a mixture of brands but most in that area were Anson cattle. Occasionally he would cut a steer out of a bunch just to give the horse some experience, but he did not like to race the stock around too much. They were in good condition but would need to be with winter approaching. The horses that showed talent at cutting would bring higher prices if sold for ranch use.

It was pleasant riding in the mountain meadows where the autumn colours were coming to the trees lining the creek banks and on the higher slopes below the darker green of the pines that bordered the canyon walls. Like everyone else in the district, Clem was sure that Jack Craig was out of the area. His only worry was how long his current job would last. Randy had told him little of the new owner's plans for the ranch, but he was spending much more time in town on legal business and had been away for longer than was his stated intention.

Clem liked the area and the ranch people he had met and would have preferred to stay around but jobs were getting scarce as the ranches reduced their staff numbers to winter levels. He was thinking that when his present job closed he would have to head to a warmer climate, where camping out would not be quite so cold. The novelty was starting to wear off the wandering life he had been leading and the prospect of staying in the one place was gradually looking more attractive.

For a girl like Maryanne Harris he would be prepared to take his chances on a more settled existence, but then he promptly dismissed such ideas again. He did not even have a steady job, let alone a proper home to offer a wife. The notion seemed even more impractical when he considered how little time they had spent together. *Get those ideas out of your head*, he told himself.

Craig had seen no riders in the area for several days and at night he had even allowed himself the luxury of a well-concealed fire. He had used up most of the canned goods and was reasonably sure that any searchers were no longer in the area. It was time to be moving again. He cooked the last of the bacon and made himself some leathery, flour-and-water Johnny cakes. These he stowed in a saddle-bag. The other bag contained spare ammunition, matches and cigarette makings. Then he rolled a blanket in a canvas pack cover and fastened it with rope to form an improvised sling. He knew that travelling would be hard and he would see more dinnertimes than dinners but he was working to a successful formula. Jack Craig might soon disappear but he would survive.

Though a stranger to the area, Craig was aware of its general geography, where all water eventually ran to the east. He would avoid the few trails that could be guarded and strike out cross-country. In a couple of days' walking he was sure that he could find another horse, and eventually the opportunity to steal another saddle would arise. He had two saddles in his hideout but they had only been taken to confuse the hunters. He would take a bridle but had no intention of lugging forty pounds of saddle.

Another day passed and Randy had not returned

from Jackson's Creek. Clem began to wonder whether he might have gone on a bender. He had seen many similar cases when men from isolated areas suddenly hit town after experiencing a liquor drought. But Clem did not worry; it was not as if things were busy at the ranch.

With unemployment looming he made a point of bringing in Rusty and Slingshot, his pack horse. The animal had earned his name by throwing riders but was happy enough to carry a pack. Each day he fed them some oats to keep them used to the grain. Oats could cause gripes with horses not used to them but they were a great source of nutrition and energy.

Randy had seriously disapproved of Clem's daily visits to the oat bin but one coffee can of grain per day for each horse was hardly likely to affect the ranch's profitability.

Clem's charges were now well-behaved and his real work with them was done, so he rode about the ranch and the nearby open range, keeping an eye out for cattle in distress. But the stock were not his only concern. He had a hunch that Craig might still be in the vicinity. Theories abounded among the neighbours as to the killer's whereabouts but all seemed to agree that he was now far away. They were probably right, Clem told himself, but one aspect still troubled him.

The camping equipment that Carr had found to be missing included a frying pan and a coffee pot as well as a large tin dish. These were not items that could be packed easily on a riding saddle, yet Craig had not taken the Box C pack saddle. If, as some thought, he had been joined by another rider the missing items would still be awkward to carry. Was Craig really intending to use them camping or had they been taken just to create confusion? A fugitive would be expected to travel light. The more he thought of the situation, the more Clem was convinced that Craig was so far proving himself to be smarter than his hunters.

Every morning he counted the horses in the pasture and checked the fence for any breaks, but all was in order. There were other ranches closer to the place where the posse had lost the trail and it was logical that Craig would be sighted there if he was still lurking in the area.

Clem's mount for the morning ride was a chunky brown horse that was developing into a very good walker. Such animals were popular choices for travellers and a swift, comfortable walk would cancel out the animal's rather plain appearance when it went for sale.

The dew was still on the grass and it gleamed knee-deep to the horse in the early morning sun. The grass was criss-crossed with tracks caused by animals moving around at night but these told the rider nothing. In the sun's heat the bent grass would straighten and next morning there would be other tracks. Clem saw nothing unusual although he had never completely relaxed. A man who spent so much time working with fresh horses would be a fool to do so. He had to appear relaxed to put his mount at ease but at the same time had to remain alert for anything that might frighten the horse into a violent, unexpected reaction.

The country was mostly rolling grassy, ridges running east from the main range of the Rockies. Dark-green pine forest clothed the rising ground to the west but the lower ground was mostly open, with the odd clumps of trees along the many small creeks in the area.

Ahead, to the north, Clem saw movement and the tiny figure of a distant rider appeared briefly on a small hill before descending into a hollow again. He turned his horse into the shade of a large pine and waited. The rider was headed his way. Just as a precaution, he loosened his Colt in its holster as he sat there.

FIFTEEN

Maryanne saw no reason to stay at home that morning. Like everyone else she was sure that Craig was miles away with no intention of returning to her locality. A couple of hours' riding about and checking any Harris cattle she saw was always enjoyable. At that time of day there was still plenty of activity among the wildlife and she saw rabbits, foxes, coyotes and antelope regularly. Occasionally she would disturb a small herd of mustangs. They would trot away in single file with an old mare leading and a weedy little stallion bringing up the rear. A couple of times she had seen a bear or a mountain lion and for that reason had a big Remington .50 calibre, single-shot pistol in a holster attached to her saddle. She did not like to shoot anything but reasoned that the noise of her father's pistol would be sufficient to scare away any dangerous animals. Though an innovation when it first became available because it fired metallic cartridges, the revolvers that came on sale

114

a couple of years later quickly pushed the single-shot weapon into obsolescence. It was accurate and hit hard but Maryanne had never had to use it except for a couple of practice shots.

Guns were the last thing on her mind though, until there was a bang and something whistled past her head. Involuntarily she jumped and that was all the startled pony needed to make it bolt. Any thoughts that the shot was accidental were quickly dispelled when she felt the animal shudder as a second bullet struck home. The pony was running away from the shooter and Maryanne let it run. She made no attempt to see who was shooting at her but knew she had to get far away as quickly as she could.

The horse began to falter. 'Keep going, Joey,' she begged. 'Just keep going.'

Clem heard the shooting and saw the rider suddenly galloping towards him. The horse was lurching in its stride and appeared to be hit. A puff of dust and another report showed that the shooter had not given up but the rider was getting out of the range of his carbine.

Then Clem saw that the rider was Maryanne. He jumped his horse into a gallop and raced toward her. 'Maryanne – over here.'

The girl looked up to see a rider approaching her, shouting as he came. At first she thought she had run into a trap but then she recognized Clem. Just as she steered towards him, her pony collapsed. She threw herself sideways in an attempt to get clear; it was a bruising landing but she rolled until she was well away from the dying animal.

Clem arrived on the scene and swung his mount between the girl and whoever was shooting at her. The shots had come from a distant edge of a pine thicket but he could not see the man behind the rifle. He was not carrying his carbine and the six-shooter would be little use at the range involved.

Maryanne scrambled to her feet and ran to where her horse was thrashing about in pain. One glance told her that her beloved pony would not be getting up again and in a mixture of grief and anger, she grabbed the big pistol from her saddle.

'Are you hurt?' Clem called. No answer came and he dismounted quickly, for he saw what she intended doing with the gun. From experience he knew that killing a horse with one shot was not as easy as many thought. 'I'd better do that. I know how to hit the right spot. You hold my horse and keep him between us and that gunman. Keep watch in case he tries to come closer.'

He doubted that Maryanne was capable of keeping watch because he suspected that her eyes would be filled with tears. He knew how it hurt to lose a good horse.

One shot later he turned to where the girl was staring across his saddle at the distant tree line. The tears were rolling down her cheeks.

'He's gone,' Clem said gently. 'Now we have to see what happens next. Keep behind my horse. But he mightn't be much shelter if that sneaking coyote changes position.'

Suddenly a series of shots echoed around the hill-sides. But this time the weapon's report was that of a six-shooter and not a rifle.

'Someone else's there,' Maryanne said in alarm. She had just finished reloading the big pistol.

'But at least they're not shooting at us. We'll just sit tight for a while and see what happens.'

Several minutes passed and a rider emerged from the trees not far from where the pair waited. It was Randy. He had a drawn revolver in his hand and was looking about warily.

'Randy,' Maryanne called and waved.

The tall rider turned his horse towards them and holstered his gun. 'What in the blazes is going on here? I heard shooting and rode to see what was happening. Suddenly someone came charging out of the trees. It must have been his shots I heard. His rifle was in its saddle scabbard but he took a shot at me with a six-shooter as he took off. I drew my gun and fired back but we both missed. He kept going and I rode over here to see who he was shooting at.'

'He was shooting at me but he hit my horse, Joey, instead. He's like a mad dog. What sort of threat was I to him?'

Randy scowled and, with a note of anger in his voice, said, 'I seem to remember that murdering devil Craig shot two old folks tied to chairs. They weren't any threat to him either. He's crazy and the sooner he's run down the better.' He pointed towards the horse that Clem had been riding. 'Take Clem's horse and I'll take you home. One of your ranch hands can bring it back later for Clem.'

Clem disagreed. 'That might not be a good idea. It's likely that Craig is somewhere between here and the Harris ranch. Maryanne might not be so lucky if she runs into him again. For some reason he seemed determined to shoot her. You know all the short cuts and can get help the quickest. We'll wait here where it seems safer until you send horses and a couple more riders back. Then we might be able to pick up that madman's trail.'

Randy might have argued but Maryanne told him firmly, 'That's the best idea, Randy. You know this country and are the best one to go for help. We'll be safe here until we get another horse.'

'I guess you're right. I'll be back as soon as I can.' Randy wheeled his horse and cantered away.

Clem pointed to a shady spot about a hundred yards away. 'Take my horse and go over there in the shade. I'll just pull the gear off your horse and follow you.'

Still upset over the attempt on her life that had cost her a treasured pony, Maryanne felt almost relieved as she led Clem's mount away to a place where she would no longer see the grim sight.

Clem undid the cinch and dragged it out from under the carcass to free the saddle. Then he collected the bridle and blanket and lugged all over to where the girl waited.

He dumped the gear on the ground and squatted nearby with his back against a tree. He was still fumbling for words to start a conversation when Maryanne told him, 'I think we will be here for a couple of hours before Randy gets back. It's lucky he came along when he did.'

Clem agreed but one thought kept coming into his mind. Who was Maryanne's recent attacker? Most likely it was Craig but Randy had never seen him, so he could not identify the hunted man. Then there was the suspicion held by some that the outlaw had an ally.

The girl seemed to have no doubts. 'I'm getting sick of being shot at,' she said. 'I can't understand why Craig would want to kill me. He could not have been after my horse because he had one when he shot at Randy.'

'Yours might have been better.'

'That could be it. But they had horses when I was shot at as I approached Anson's. I could see horses in the corral and a buckboard team and a saddled Appaloosa horse at the back of the house.'

Clem looked at her sharply, 'Are you sure you saw an Appaloosa?'

'It was an Appaloosa. I couldn't see it all but I saw the white blanket on its rump. I looked for it when the posse brought back the stolen horses but it must have been the one killed in the attack on the Dibley ranch.'

'That horse was a black one. I saw it. The only Appaloosa on the Anson ranch was Randy's and he was riding it when he came to find me.'

Maryanne frowned. 'I might have seen that horse on my second visit to the Ansons. So much happened that day that I probably got mixed up. Randy wouldn't shoot at me. I've known him for years.'

'Were you sweethearts?' Clem had asked the question without thinking and then realized that it was none of his business.

'No. We've always been friends, but Randy is not my type.'

For some reason Clem felt relieved by that admission. He continued, 'I wasn't expecting Randy to show up here. I thought he was still in Jackson's Creek. He's been spending a lot of time there lately.'

'There is a bridle trail from town not far from here and it is a short cut to our ranches. If Randy was coming home on that trail he would have been close enough to hear those shots. If he had arrived a little earlier, he might have caught Craig in the act.'

'He might have got his head blown off too. Craig is as cunning as they come and he's mighty dangerous. It might just be coincidence that you were shot at twice but I suggest you don't go riding alone until we run him down.'

SIXTEEN

Craig was always suspicious when he heard shooting. It was hard to tell where the shots had come from because of the way they echoed about the hills and canyons, but he reckoned they were not far away. Experience told him that the first reports could have been someone hunting but the second round of shots had been from a revolver and few men hunted with six-shooters. Warily, like a much-hunted animal, he made his way down a brushy ridge, keeping under cover and studying the landscape around him as he went. Visibility, though, was limited because of the tall pines on the lower slopes. At every patch of open ground, he would remain in the brush and look about until he was as satisfied as he could be that nobody was lurking in the timber on the other side.

Eventually the trees started to thin and he could see a wide expanse of green grass showing between the trunks ahead. As he came closer he saw that it was a couple of hundred yards wide and then the trees started again. He would have to be very watchful before he risked crossing such an exposed area. It would not do to be caught on foot in the open.

He had almost reached the edge of the trees when he heard a horse snort. Craig froze instantly. It was not the snort of a mustang stallion challenging an intruder. The snort came from upwind of where he was so he was sure that the animal had not scented him. His hopes rose. He needed a horse but had not expected to find one at such an isolated place. Finding it, however, was only part of the problem. The animal, if it was a stray, still had to be caught and then ridden. Very cautiously he crept to the edge of the tree line.

Craig was far from Clem's mind as he relaxed in the shade and tried to make casual conversation with Maryanne. She had been badly shaken by the attempt on her life and he was trying to get her emotions settled as best he could. Not being greatly experienced in such matters he was having difficulty finding the right words. He was torn between a serious and sympathetic approach and a humorous one in an attempt to lighten her mood. In the end he settled for a serious approach.

'Maybe you should have gone with Randy,' he said. 'You would get home a lot sooner.'

'No. It was safer for all concerned that I stayed here. That person seems to be after me and he is somewhere down the trail between here and home. For all we know he could have an ambush somewhere along the way he knows we would have to go. I don't want someone else getting killed protecting me.'

'In both cases the shooter was a fair distance away. He might not have known who he was shooting at.'

Maryanne disagreed. 'The shots fired at me the day the Ansons were murdered were from a fair way away but the gunman was closer today. We were going through a bit of rough ground and Joey was constantly changing direction. I think that was why he missed.' Then, for the first time, she smiled. 'He's had a bit of target practice at me now. I hope his aim doesn't improve.'

'I hope he doesn't come back. I should have borrowed Randy's Winchester but I didn't think of it at the time.'

'He might think Randy is still with us and that now the odds are too long for him.'

Clem had removed the saddle and bridle from his horse and was letting it graze on the end of a lariat when he noticed that the rope was likely to be caught on Maryanne's saddle. He climbed to his feet, picked up the saddle, and went to move it to a more convenient place. He had it in both hands when he heard a man's voice.

'Nobody move.'

A bearded, dirty man emerged from the trees

with a Winchester carbine pointed at Clem.

Craig ignored Maryanne and seeing that her companion had a saddle in both hands, he relaxed a little and took a couple of cautious steps forward. From that angle, though, he could not see the big Remington pistol attached to the saddle.

Clem recognized Craig immediately and, given the number of murders attributed to the Dole gang, he took a desperate chance. He grabbed the pistol and dropped the saddle. The outlaw was taken by surprise because he knew that Clem's hand was nowhere near his six-shooter and he was trying to watch two people at once. His eye caught Clem's sudden movement and saw a gun appear in his hand as if by magic. As Craig saw the big .50-calibre bore swinging towards him he fired a hasty shot, but did not shoot quickly or accurately enough. The 265-grain Remington bullet smashed his left arm and almost tore the rifle from his grasp. A body hit would have knocked Craig down, but the arm wound spun him around and sent him reeling. Unable to work the rifle's action any more, he dropped it and reached for his revolver.

Clem had already discarded the empty pistol and was first to get his gun clear of the holster. Craig, still unbalanced from the bullet's impact, made no attempt to swap lead with him but staggered back behind a tree. Clem's shot knocked a piece of bark off the trunk but missed his target. As he cocked the weapon for the next shot, Craig moved again, darting to another tree. He emerged briefly to fire a shot, but it appeared to be more of a warning for Clem to keep his distance.

Maryanne crouched low and ran across to Craig's fallen rifle. She scooped it up and ran a few more yards to where a fallen pine tree offered a bit of cover.

Craig saw the movement and sent a shot in her direction, but in doing so partly exposed himself to Clem. Clem's gun roared. More bark flew from the edge of the tree trunk but the bullet also grazed the man sheltering behind it. He flinched and momentarily gave Maryanne the opportunity for a shot. She was not used to snap-shooting and her bullet missed, but Craig reeled back. He was being fired upon from two different angles and the tree was not wide enough to protect him from both. He had another problem, too. With his left arm broken, he could not reload his gun. Retreat was his only option and he darted from behind his tree in an attempt to run deeper into the timber. He had barely moved two paces when Clem's shot took him in the neck, smashing his spine and tumbling him into the long grass.

'Keep down, Maryanne. Stay there.' Clem had seen the gun fly from Craig's hand as he fell but was not inclined to take chances with such a dangerous opponent. With his gun cocked he advanced slowly, keeping the sights aligned on the fallen man. His precautions though, were quickly proved unnecessary. The bullet, after hitting Craig's spine, had been deflected into the base of his skull. Craig was probably dead before he hit the ground.

'Don't come over here, Maryanne. He's finished. It's Jack Craig, the last of the Dole gang. It's all over now. I'm sorry you saw all this, It might have been better if you had gone back with Randy. He was keen for you to go and as things have turned out I think he was right.'

The girl shook her head. 'Call it a woman's intuition, but I felt I should have stayed with you and it's lucky I did, otherwise you wouldn't have surprised him with that pistol that was on my saddle.'

'I was glad to have you on my side. You took a big chance picking up that rifle, but you made all the difference when you did. Craig was caught in a crossfire.'

'Surely you didn't expect me to scream and faint? If someone wants to kill me I'll make them work to do it.'

Clem looked about and sighted the canvas roll and saddle-bags that Craig must have dropped before he confronted them. He picked them up and carried them back to where the very pale-faced girl was now sitting shivering on a log. Her confident, determined manner was suddenly gone. 'How do you feel now?'

'Awful. For all my tough talk a while ago, I can't seem to stop shaking.'

'That's normal. You have just come through a bad experience that most folks never have. I've seen big, strong men shake worse than that after surviving a close-range gunfight.'

'You don't seem to be worried.'

'Looks can fool you. Inside I'm feeling pretty churned up and I know I'll have trouble sleeping tonight. Killing people ain't something I could get used to.'

'I was there when you shot Vern Black, but have you killed someone else before?'

'I had to,' Clem admitted. 'I worked on a ranch that got involved in a range war. There was a lot of shooting and my side lost. Only two of us got out alive and I left New Mexico in a hurry. The winners owned the law as well as the range and I didn't fancy waiting around to be hit with a murder charge. I never shot a man who wasn't trying to kill me at the time but it's marvellous how some people can twist the law. I hope it don't make you uneasy being stuck out here with such a desperate character.'

The girl gave a quick smile. 'I don't think you are too bad a character, Clem. As long as I've known you, I haven't seen anything I would criticize.'

'That's nice to know.' He pointed to Craig's saddle-bags. 'I reckon we'll find the Anson cattle money in there, but let's leave it till the others arrive so there'll be witnesses to whatever we find. If the count comes up short I don't want us being blamed for taking some of it.'

'Surely people wouldn't think that we'd do such a thing?'

'Don't bet on it. When large heaps of money go missing a lot of folks with nothing better to do will sit around and blame all sorts of innocent parties.'

Maryanne remained unconvinced but curbed her curiosity. They moved away from where Craig lay and found a comfortable spot in the shade.

Jud Harris found them there half an hour later when he arrived accompanied by Randy and two well-armed cowhands, one of whom was leading a spare horse.

SEVENTEEN

Relief showed on the rancher's normally stern face as he saw his daughter rise to her feet and hurry to greet him. He threw himself from the saddle and hugged her to him. 'Thank God you're all right. Randy said there was a bit of shooting here. What happened?'

'Someone tried to kill me but the bullet killed Joey instead. Luckily Clem came along and scared him off.'

'He had a couple of shots at me just after that,' Randy interrupted. 'It must have been Jack Craig.'

'It wasn't Craig,' Clem declared.

Harris turned toward the speaker and demanded, 'Why not?'

'Because Craig is lying dead over there in the trees. Maryanne and I had a gun battle with him. He lost. He came out of the trees and stuck us up while we were waiting around. I think he was after my horse.'

'Why in the hell didn't you just give it to him rather than put my daughter at risk? Horses are cheap.'

'Craig left too many dead people behind him. We know he killed that line rider and he was part of the gang that murdered the Ansons. There was no guarantee he would have left us alive. I had a chance and I took it. Maryanne took a hand at the right time and we were lucky.'

'That's the end of the gang,' Randy said in a satisfied tone. 'It's all over now.'

Clem had other ideas. 'Not quite. Who was it shot at you? It couldn't have been Craig because he had no horse.'

'And there's still the matter of the Ansons' money,' Harris reminded.

Pointing to where the dead man lay, Clem said, 'He was carrying a bit of stuff. It's over there. We decided not to look at it until there were a few more witnesses.'

He walked over to where the dead man's blanket roll and saddle-bags lay. Picking them up he returned to the others and dropped them on the ground. 'This is all Craig was carrying. Does someone want to open it up?'

Randy volunteered. He knelt eagerly and unbuckled the saddle-bags. There was some spare ammunition, tobacco and a small amount of what looked like very unappetizing food. He inverted the bags to be sure he had not overlooked anything, then looked up at the others. 'There's no money here. It must be in his bedroll.'

But the roll contained only a coat, a bridle and a blanket.

Harris studied the killer's few possessions before suggesting, 'The money might be on him. Did you search him, Clem?'

'No. There's blood everywhere and I thought I'd leave that job to someone who had a bigger stake in this business.'

'Don't look at me,' Randy protested. 'It might be my folks' money but he wouldn't carry it on him. Uncle Bert liked his money in gold coins. There'd be more than a man could comfortably carry in his pocket. I reckon that whoever took the money stashed it somewhere and with the whole gang gone, who knows where it is? Chances are it will never be found. Harry Anson won't be happy about losing that much *dinero* but he has plenty.'

Harris gave a grunt that was his version of a relieved sigh. 'Thank God this mess is all over and I can get back to ranching.'

'I'm not so sure it is all over,' Clem said. 'There's been a lot of strange business happening and some of it don't make sense.'

Harris was in no mood to argue. 'We ain't lawmen. Let's cover up this feller's carcass and leave Weatherby to tie up any loose ends. I'll send one of my riders to town with the news.'

One of the cowhands saddled Maryanne's horse

while Harris and Clem wrapped Craig's body in the blanket and canvas sheet he had been carrying. They secured the bundle with rope and piled branches over it to discourage scavenging animals. Then the group mounted and left the scene.

When they reached the Harris ranch all were invited in for refreshments but then Randy remembered that he had left a couple of horses in the corral and was not sure that there was enough water for them in the trough. The day had been an unseasonally hot one, so reluctantly he declined the invitation.

Clem had secretly felt that Randy's standard of horse care left much to be desired and saw no reason for two men to be doing a one-man job that he would prefer to do himself anyway. 'There's no need for two of us to let out those horses,' he said. 'You stop off here and I'll keep going. There's a couple of horses that I want to have a good look at while it is still daylight. I might need to pull the shoes off one.'

'That's fine by me. There are a couple of things I need to talk to Jud about. I'll be along a bit later.'

As he turned his horse away Clem thought he saw a disappointed look flash across Maryanne's face. That's only wishful thinking, he told himself.

Back at the Anson ranch he found that the trough had indeed been dry so he turned the three horses in the corral back into the pasture where they could graze and drink from the stream. He inspected one of the animals going for sale and decided that come the next day he would trim its feet. Another with only two loose shoes left he brought to the corral. He quickly removed the shoes and trimmed the hoofs with hoof-nippers and a rasp. It was simple work but hard on his back, so Clem decided he had done enough for that day.

Only one more task remained. Rusty was standing at the gate, waiting for his small nightly ration of oats. Clem went to the feed bin and, with the old coffee can scooped up a quantity of grain which he then transferred to an ancient tin dish. On the second scoop the can hit something metallic that was buried in the grain. Expecting to find another tin-can scoop, he felt down under the oats. His fingers encountered something entirely different. His idle curiosity turned to surprise when he unearthed what he had found. At first he was shocked, but the find suddenly resolved some of the doubts that had been creeping into his mind.

He was preparing their evening meal of beef and potatoes done in a Dutch oven when Randy came home. His day had been a long one and he was very tired.

Later, as they ate, the pair discussed the day's happenings. They speculated upon the identity of the mysterious rider who had shot at both Maryanne and Randy but Clem could offer no enlightenment there. He was a stranger in the district and knew little about people on the other ranches.

'I think I have figured it out,' Randy announced. 'Craig was to meet someone around that place where he was hiding. Whoever it was must have panicked when he saw other people there, and he took shots at them. Maybe he was only firing to scare us away.'

'He sure scared Maryanne. Having a horse shot from under you is more than a bit scary.'

'You sound like you're speaking from experience.'

'I am, but it's something I don't talk about,' Clem admitted.

Randy looked hard at him and concern showed on his face. 'You ain't wanted by the law, are you?'

'No, I'm not. But that's all I'm going to say. Now finish your grub and I'll wash up. Is there anything special you want me to do tomorrow?'

'Just give those horses plenty of work. Three days from now we'll be driving them to town. There's a horse auction on Saturday. And just while I think of it, don't feed them any oats. We don't want them bucking their brands off. There are plenty of horses around this county and they are dirt cheap because they're so badly trained. I want this ranch to show a good profit on our horses because they have been trained properly. Harry Anson might be a miserable sonofabitch but I don't want him saying that I didn't do the best for this ranch while I've been running it.'

'So my job is coming to an end?'

'I reckon so. Harry Anson told me to pay you up when the horses are delivered for sale. I'm to stay here until he finds a buyer for the ranch and then I'll be out of a job too.'

Clem was tired but slept badly that night. The day's happenings were still flashing through his mind and he found it hard to relax. The more he thought about events, the more questions arose. He was certain that Black's obsession with capturing the last of the Dole gang was based on more than righteous indignation, but that seemed to have little bearing on the presesnt situation.

The latest discovery had caused him to start reconsidering his previous ideas. Gradually he was coming to the conclusion that somebody had deliberately tried to kill Maryanne, but the reasoning behind this was still obscure.

Just before he eventually drifted off to sleep Clem decided that he would visit the Harris ranch. He would need to be discreet in making his enquiries but he weighed the risk to someone's reputation against the girl's life and had no trouble deciding which was more important. Ideally it would be better if he spoke to the girl alone and he was still trying to think of how to do this when he fell asleep.

EIGHTEEN

Clem and Randy had split the cooking duties between them. Randy had little culinary imagination and was happy to stick to the more conventional breakfast. Clem, however, had been looking after himself for much longer and had found several ways to vary what was basically a meat-and-potatoes evening meal.

'What's on the programme for today?' Clem asked as he sat down to the usual bacon-and-eggs breakfast. Their bread supply had run out several days before so toast was off the menu until someone went to town again.

'It might be best if you took a ride over to that timbered country to the south when you are working the horses. I think that cattle might be feeding through the pines there and drifting off the range. They will need to be rounded up for sale and we don't want to miss stock that have strayed. Turn back any you see and look for signs that there might

136

be more about.'

'I'll take that roan gelding today. He'd enjoy a bit of cattle work. He has the makings of a top cow horse. I'll come back at lunchtime and change horses. What are you planning to do today?'

'I haven't made up my mind yet but there's a lot of paper work that I've been neglecting. Put my Appaloosa in the corral, just in case I get sick of doing accounts and go for a ride later. I can understand why my uncle let some of the paper work build up, although I wish he hadn't. Harry is asking for all sorts of details and I'm damned if I know where to find half of what he wants. The miserable sonofabitch should get out of his Chicago office and chase it up himself.'

Clem left Randy to his account books, and as he saddled his selected mount he told himself that he would have the more enjoyable work that day. It was fine riding weather and the horse was a good one, but he was not as relaxed as he should have been. The doubts of the previous day had returned. He was some distance from the house when he decided upon a course of action. When a timbered ridge screened him from any chance of Randy seeing him he turned the roan's head and rode for the Harris ranch. If he wanted to keep his horse in good shape the round trip would take two hours and he would have to fabricate a story to cover his delay in getting back to the ranch, but questions needed to be asked.

Maryanne was helping her mother with the housework when, casually glancing through an open window, she saw Clem approaching.

Clara followed her daughter's gaze and frowned a little as she saw the cowboy dismount and secure his horse to the hitching rack. 'I wonder what he wants at this time of day? Don't tell me it's more trouble. You'd best open the door for him, Maryanne. Because he looks fit to bust it down if we don't.'

Clem was pleased to see that it was Maryanne who greeted him when the door opened. He swept off his hat but did not take time for more formality. 'Maryanne, can I talk to you alone? There are some questions I need to ask you. Is anyone else here?'

'My mother's here. Come inside.'

'I'd prefer not to. It's not something I would want other people to know at present, in case I have things wrong. Just for a short time I need you to keep a secret. Can we talk privately somewhere just for a couple of minutes?'

'I'll get my hat and we can talk while I'm feeding the chickens.'

Clara was torn between curiosity and suspicion as she saw her daughter take her hat from a peg near the door. 'What's that young fellow up to, Maryanne?'

'He wants to ask me something in private.'

Her mother's secret fears emerged with a rush. 'Don't go accepting any proposals. You hardly know him.'

138

Maryanne laughed. 'Don't worry, I'm sure it is nothing as serious as that.'

She left the house and said to Clem, 'Talk to me while I'm feeding the chickens. I'm sure they won't cackle about any secrets they might overhear.'

Clem followed her to a feed shed where she collected a small dish of wheat. 'There's something that's troubling me,' he began. 'How well do you know Randy?'

'He came here a couple of years ago and started working for his uncle and aunt. He never said anything about where he had been before that. The Ansons were a big clan in Missouri, so he probably came from there.'

'How did he get on with his kinfolks here?'

'I remember hearing Bert Anson tell Pa that Randy was forever trying to take charge. Seems he was always wanting to run things his way, but they kept him in check. Harry told me that Randy had big ideas but was only half as smart as he thought he was.'

'What sort of man is Harry Anson?'

'He is a really nice man, very kind and loving to his family. He was not cut out for ranching but always kept a close eye on his parents.'

'He wasn't mean?'

'Heavens no! We had a drought two years ago and Harry offered us a loan to see us through. We didn't take up the offer because the drought broke but we have always thought highly of Harry. Why all these questions?'

'I'll explain in a minute. Did you ever see Bert Anson with a cash-box when you visited the ranch?'

'Yes, I did. It was a bronze-coloured tin box that sat on his writing desk. He often used to joke that there wasn't much in it. But a couple of months ago he did well at the cattle sales. Pa said that the box was missing when they were cleaning up after the Dole gang's raid. They probably took it.'

'They didn't. I found it empty yesterday.'

'So they only took the money. Where did you find it?'

'I found it hidden in a bin of oats in the Ansons' feed shed. Mickey Dole would not have bothered to hide an empty box.'

Maryanne's eyes widened in surprise as she realized the implication of Clem's discovery. 'Oh no,' she gasped. 'Do you think Randy stole it?'

'He might have and he might have even killed the Ansons after Dole had left.'

The girl's voice was a mixture of shock and disbelief as she said, 'I can't imagine Randy would do such a thing.'

Clem continued. 'You thought you saw an Appaloosa horse in the ranch yard just before someone fired at you, but later I suggested that you might have seen it while Randy and I were there. I think you were right.'

'I was having a few doubts because I thought someone fired three shots at me, but I might have been confused with all that happened that day. Pa said they only found two bullet shells outside the window and there was no other one inside the room, so now I am not sure of that.'

'Three shots were fired. Randy loaned me his rifle to take out with the posse. He had left the third empty shell in the breech to guard against the gun going off accidentally. It's a good safety measure when carrying rifles on horseback.'

'Do you think Randy tried to kill me?'

'The first time he might have only wanted to scare you off, but then he must have had second thoughts. I think he tried again the other day when your horse was shot. He was the only one who saw the mysterious gunman who shot at you and him. Then Craig walked into the middle of things and conveniently created a diversion.'

'I wonder what would have happened if I had taken up his offer to escort me home,' Maryanne said.

Clem's face was grim. 'Chances are that he would have shot you and blamed it on that mystery gunman.'

The girl was not convinced. She frowned and shook her head. 'But I've known Randy for years. It's hard to believe.'

'I think that Randy killed his folks after the Dole gang left the ranch. He knew his uncle had that money, so he shot both the Ansons when he found them tied to chairs. It was easy to take the money and blame Dole but then he saw you coming. He fired a few shots to scare you off and then went to find me. Later he realized that you might have seen too much, although you didn't know it at the time. He tried to kill you in case you mentioned something that set people thinking.'

'Can you prove any of this?'

'I'll have a good try. Meanwhile I want you to keep close to the ranch here. Don't go out riding alone or go anywhere with Randy. Don't tell your ma and pa and just keep it a secret until I am really sure. Then I'll get in touch with Weatherby and let the law handle things.'

'Weatherby came through here this morning. Pa's taking him up to where we left Craig. They should be back here about sundown. Our two hands are with them too. Should I send him to the Anson place?'

'It might be a good idea. As a lawman he would want to know about that empty cash box and Randy will sure have some explaining to do. Weatherby should be able to find out whether Randy is a murderer or just a thief. I have to go now. Just tell Weatherby I want to see him urgently and be careful not to show yourself outside any more than you need to. That mystery gunman might not miss next time.'

NINETEEN

Clem rode hard and was not too late getting back to the ranch, but his horse showed signs of hard usage that could not be disguised. The dried sweat and drooping head advertised that the animal had been engaged in a fair bit of travelling. He had returned by a circuitous route so that he approached the ranch from the direction Randy would have expected. Hoping that he would not be observed, he unsaddled his mount and rubbed its back to break up the sweat. Absorbed by this task, he did not hear Randy come up behind him.

'You used that horse pretty hard,' the other accused. The disapproval in his voice evident.

Clem thought quickly. 'I had a bit of trouble with a couple of old mossy horns that objected to being turned back, and later there was a cow that had hidden a new calf somewhere. She kept breaking back to where she had left it. I followed her back but couldn't find the calf. She wasn't going to it

143

while I was about. In the end I decided it was a waste of time as the calf might not have been able to travel anyway.'

Randy nodded as though in agreement, and in a friendlier tone he said, 'When you go out again later, go straight south for a couple of miles and then chase up any cattle you meet on the way back. I need to get a good idea of whether many have strayed in that direction. Harry Anson always wants to know the full picture. He writes just about every week – doesn't trust me, the miserable sonofabitch.'

Clem thought that Harry had the right idea but said nothing.

Randy continued: 'When you go out later I'll go some of the way with you. There's a bit of fence closing off a bad gully and I want to make sure that it's still there after that heavy rain last week.'

Both men had a quick meal and went out to saddle their horses, Clem noted with growing unease that Randy had attached a rifle to his saddle, 'Figuring on doing a bit of hunting, Randy?'

'Maybe. Chances are I might get a shot at a coyote and that two-legged skunk that took a few shots at me the other day might still be around. Don't forget about him.'

Clem had forgotten because he was sure that the man did not exist.

The pair rode out together and it was obvious that Randy had something on his mind. Never very talkative, he was even quieter than usual and Clem found himself making most of the conversation. He positioned himself on Randy's left and allowed his horse to walk about half a length behind his companion's fast-walking mount. It was a position that placed the leading rider at a disadvantage if he should suddenly go for a gun.

'That horse ain't walking very well,' Randy observed and there was a note of disapproval in his voice. 'It ain't right that a man can't ride in place where he can talk to others. Injuns might trail along behind each other but with white men it's downright unsociable.'

'He's not too bad,' Clem replied, 'but he can't walk like that horse of yours and I don't want to spoil him by making him jog to keep up. Given a bit more time his walking should improve.'

He did not know whether Randy accepted that explanation but had no intention of putting himself in a position of disadvantage. He had been deliberately slowing the horse's pace.

Randy pointed to a gully that crossed their path and ran down the sloping ground to their left, cutting deeper as it went. 'This is where I leave you. I'll see you back at the ranch about sundown.' He turned his mount across in front of Clem and started riding down the hill.

With a sense of relief Clem rode on. For a short while he thought that Randy was no longer a problem. Then some inbuilt caution reminded him of the rifle the other had been carrying. He glanced back over his shoulder.

Randy had dismounted and was aiming the Winchester at him.

Clem wheeled his mount sideways to throw off Randy's aim and hit its flanks with the spurs. The first shot passed close enough for him to feel its draught. Another shot missed by a wider margin as he urged the horse towards a distant clump of trees, then suddenly changed direction again. Randy would expect him to seek cover in the timber but Clem had no intention of riding into the other's sights. He decided that his chances would be better with a fast retreat out of range. Beyond 200 yards he had a good chance of escaping unscathed.

The long grass partially concealed the prairie dog village; by the time horse and rider saw the bare earth around the holes, they were in it. The pony crashed down, throwing its rider some distance out ahead of it. Clem saw the ground coming up to meet him and instinctively reached out with his hands turned in to avoid breaking his arms as they broke his fall. He hit the ground and rolled, hoping that he was clear of the horse, but he need not have worried because he had scarcely stopped rolling when the animal regained its feet and took off. A bullet kicked a spurt of dirt into Clem's face as he rolled again seeking cover. This time he fell into a shallow erosion gully, which provided a slight degree of cover from Randy's position, but gave him little protection from other angles.

His horse slowed to a trot a hundred yards away as the long split reins began to catch around its legs, but it might as well have been on the moon for all the good that would do its erstwhile rider.

Clem removed his hat and peered above the grass, half expecting to feel the impact of a bullet. But his luck was holding because Randy was mounting his horse.

Any relief though was short-lived. Randy cantered almost casually around him in a wide arc until he reached the loose horse. He was cutting his target off from any escape routes.

Aiming high and hoping he had the right elevation, Clem tried a shot from his Colt.

'You'll have to do better that that,' Randy jeered as he caught the loose horse's reins and led it further away. 'I'll be back for you in a minute.'

He led Clem's horse a further hundred yards, dropped the reins again and galloped back, halting just out of accurate revolver range. 'You thought you were smart,' he taunted. 'I knew you had found that cash-box because it had been moved. When I hid it I placed it in a certain way so I'd know if it had been disturbed.'

Clem shouted back, 'Did you kill the Ansons?'

'You can ask them when you catch up with them next.' To punctuate his remarks and to show off his advantage, Randy sprayed a few more rifle shots in Clem's direction.

Clem crouched lower in the shallow depression

as one bullet kicked up dirt in front of him and two more struck just behind him. Sooner or later he knew that Randy would get just the right point of aim. Hoping to lure his attacker closer, Clem made no reply but replaced the spent cartridge in his gun and waited.

Seconds dragged by, then he heard the sound of his opponent's horse circling to his left, moving higher up the gradually sloping ground to a point where its rider could overlook his refuge. Clem knew that he only had seconds to find more cover.

Randy rode around the slope, rifle at the ready, his eyes glued on the area where he knew that his target was concealed. Absently he took his last two rifle cartridges from the pocket of his leather vest and slipped them into the Winchester's magazine. He had not been counting his shots, but he knew that the rifle had not been empty, so he was reasonably confident that he would have enough bullets to finish the fight he had started.

The antagonists saw each other simultaneously, but Clem had been waiting and fired first. The shot missed, though it passed close enough to Randy's horse to frighten the animal. It jumped forward, spoiling its rider's aim and moving him to an awkward angle for shooting back. Randy fired anyway but did no execution. Cursing, he brought the horse under control and wheeled it back for another shot.

Clem broke cover and ran for a log on the

ground about thirty yards away. It was old and rotten and he was not sure that it would stop a rifle bullet, but there was no other option.

Randy saw him and snapped a shot at him, but a moving horse is a difficult base for rifle shooting. He tried again and the bullet thumped solidly into the log, once more missing its intended mark. Swearing under his breath, the rifleman jumped from his horse, dropped to one knee and fired another shot. This one sent a chunk of wood flying from the top of the log and again a revolver shot came back at him. By then, though, he was treating his opponent with disdain. Accurate long-range shooting with the short-barrelled revolver was so difficult that the odds were well and truly on his side. He fired another shot to keep Clem's head down and began to walk even closer to a slightly rising piece of ground that would allow him to see over the log.

Clem needed no telling about the perilous situation he was in, He had managed to fully load his gun again but found he had only three spare cartridges left in his belt. To survive he had to finish the battle in nine shots. Somehow he had to lure Randy into more effective range but did not know how he could. Because he was forced to stay under cover he was losing track of Randy's exact location and was in no position to reply effectively to the rifle shots.

Another bullet thudded into the log and soon it

would be no protection at all because in a few more strides the rifleman would be able to see over it. Since he had dismounted his mobility would be slower but his shooting was bound to improve.

Clem took a chance. He jumped to his feet and sprinted towards his adversary. As the Winchester came to Randy's shoulder, Clem threw himself to the ground again. The plan worked because the bullet, fired from an uphill position, went over his head. Remembering to aim high, he snapped another shot which also missed. Clem had to close the range.

The unexpected move seemed to confuse Randy who had expected that his target would try to escape. Now suddenly he was charging into pistol range.

By frantically rolling sideways Clem narrowly avoided the next bullet and rolled on to his belly with his arm outstretched for a shot. He found himself looking straight into the muzzle of Randy's rifle and was close enough to see the grim smile on the other's face. But he was not close enough to hear the click as the firing pin struck an empty chamber.

An urgent flick of the loading lever and the stunned look on Randy's face was enough to show that the rifle was somehow out of action. Clem fired and missed but bounded to his feet as he saw his adversary cast aside the empty weapon and draw his revolver.

They surged toward each other firing, as they came. Through a haze of gunsmoke Clem saw Randy reel and then recover. Sighting on Randy, Clem cocked the gun and squeezed the trigger. The sound of the hammer falling on a spent cartridge told him that he should have been counting his shots.

The faint breeze blew away the powder smoke to reveal Randy pale-faced and apparently unsteady, but still looking at him over the sights of his revolver. A red stain was growing on the left shoulder of his shirt where it showed around his leather vest. 'Your luck's out, Clem. This time you're the one caught with an empty gun. I know I have at least two slugs still in this gun. You got me in the shoulder but I'll be able to tell folks how you stole that money and tried to kill me. I'll come out of all this a hero and folks will be left wondering what you did with the money you stole.'

'That won't do you any good, Randy. Folks already know that you took the money and probably killed your relatives. Weatherby's on his way here by now.'

'That stupid . . .' Randy had gone deathly pale. He swayed on his feet, sought to retain his balance, then collapsed. He was semi-conscious when he hit the ground and the gun fell from his hand.

Clem ran forward, picked up the fallen revolver and knelt beside his would-be killer. Peeling back the leather vest he saw that Randy's shirt was soaked and dark-red arterial blood was pumping from the hole in his shoulder. Quickly he untied the fallen man's bandanna, wadded it into a ball and pressed it against the wound, but the blood still continued to flow. He was still trying to stanch the bleeding when the wounded man shuddered and went limp. Seconds later all breathing stopped and he lay still in death.

Clem climbed to his feet and stared down at the man who had tried so hard to kill him. He knew he had been lucky. Normally a shoulder wound would not be fatal but he had seen before how bullets could take strange paths when they entered a body. The fatal slug had probably hit a bone and had been deflected downward, severing an artery as it went.

'Looks like that money won't be any use to you now,' he said to the corpse before walking away to catch the two horses.

TWENTY

Harry Anson arrived a couple of days after Clem had telegraphed the news to him. He was a small, serious-looking man in his early forties, wearing a rather dusty dark suit and a derby hat. He climbed down from a hired buggy, looked at the ranch house and shook his head, as if to dispel the gloomy thoughts about all that had happened.

Clem had been expecting him and, upon hearing the wheels on the gravel, emerged from a shed where he had been rearranging the saddlery.

The newcomer saw him and extended his right hand when they met. 'I'm Harry Anson. I take it you're Clem Shaw?'

Clem was surprised at the little man's strong handshake. 'That's right. I've been keeping an eye on things until you can decide what to do. When it suits you, I'll move on.'

'There's no rush. Let's unhitch this horse and put it away and we can go into the house and talk.'

'I'll fix the horse,' Clem told him. 'You'll get your suit all dusty. Why don't you go inside and make yourself comfortable.'

Anson looked about and said, 'I'll give you a hand. Just sometimes I enjoy getting dusty again. It's strange. I couldn't wait to study law and get away from this ranch, but occasionally I find it relaxing to be back here doing something useful with my hands just for a change. It's a nice break from the courts and the office.'

Later they returned to the house and talked in the kitchen while Clem made an evening meal.

'Did you have any luck with that money?' Clem asked. 'I searched everywhere around here. I don't have any idea where Randy could have hidden it.'

'I know where it is. It's in a bank in Thomasville, fifty miles from here. A friend of mine told me that he saw Randy coming out of the bank there. When everyone thought Randy was in Jackson's Creek he had taken the stagecoach to Thomasville and opened a bank account with the money. Once the ranch was sold he did not need to hang around this area and might even have attracted attention if he did. Folks might start wondering at his sudden wealth. Away from his own locality he was just another stranger with money.'

'So you can get the money back?'

'I'm pretty sure I can,' Anson said. 'It would be easier if I had details of the account and there will be some legal hurdles to jump, but I'll get it.'

Clem suddenly remembered. 'Just on the subject of Randy, the mailman delivered a big envelope addressed to him yesterday. I'll get it for you.' He went into another room and returned with a brown envelope, which he passed to Anson. 'You'll know best what should happen to this.'

The lawyer glanced at the postmark on the envelope and started smiling. 'I thought I recognized that envelope,' he explained. 'This is from the Thomasville bank. I think we'll find that they have sent Randy the details of his new account. This should make recovery a bit easier.'

As he spoke Anson produced a pocket knife and slit open the envelope. It contained a cheque book and account details. 'This is why we found no bank details in Randy's possession. The bank was a bit late posting them to him. I'll take them back with me but I'll show them to Weatherby when I drop my buggy back to Jackson's Creek. He'll probably want to hold them but I'll bluff him out of that with a bit of legal jargon. Chances are he'd lose them if I left them with him.'

They talked until late in the night and the result was that the ranch would not be sold. Clem would manage it over winter with the option of continuing or hiring a replacement and round-up crew before the cattle work started in spring. It was an offer that he accepted with alacrity.

Next morning Anson was packing his bag when he glanced out of the bedroom window. 'Looks like we have some sort of deputation coming,' he called to Clem, who was clearing the kitchen after break-fast.

Three riders halted in front of the house, Maryanne, her father and Weatherby.

Harry went out to meet them. 'Howdy folks. Get down and come inside.'

At that point Weatherby saw Clem emerge from the house. 'Just the man I was after,' he announced.

Immediately Clem thought of the trouble he had experienced in New Mexico, but then reasoned that Maryanne and her father would not be there to back up the lawman. Suspiciously he asked, 'What's the trouble?'

The deputy seemed to enjoy the other's nervousness. 'It's about Jack Craig, that feller you shot recently.'

'What about him?'

'Turns out he wasn't Jack Craig.'

'That don't make him any deader. What's all this about?'

As though explaining to a small child, Weatherby said slowly, 'His real name was Alfred Henry Slevin. He was as bad as they come but kept disappearing and would turn up somewhere else using a different name. That made him very hard to track. He had more tricks than a mongrel hound has fleas. He would join up with other gangs in places where he was not known and then disappear for a while when he had a bit of cash behind him. There's some folks about who thought Alf Slevin died years ago. But he had a tattoo on his arm, just a very rough star but it was enough for us to start making other enquiries when we hauled in Craig's carcass. From a few other scars he was carrying, and from going through old Wanted posters, I was able to confirm who he was. Somehow Vern Black knew Slevin had joined up with Mickey Dole and was on his way to Jackson's Creek when the gang busted out of jail.'

'What does all this have to do with me?'

Weatherby smiled. 'There's a reward of two thousand dollars on his hide that folks in Texas want to pay you.'

Clem's first reaction was to refuse. He had seen what bounty hunting had done to Vern Black. Such a thought, though, was quickly dismissed when he saw Maryanne standing there and knew that he no longer wanted to be moving on.

'There were two of us involved in shooting that outlaw. It was Maryanne's shooting that drove him out of cover. She was shot at, too. Any reward should be split fifty-fifty. Would the folks in Texas agree to that?'

Predictably, Weatherby was unsure, but Harry Anson stepped in. 'I'm sure I can fix that without too much trouble and I won't charge a cent because I will be keeping in good with my neighbours and getting a new foreman at the same time.'

'I – er – suppose that would be all right.' The deputy was uncertain about any situation that was a little different from the normal run of things.

'Looks like you two will be partners,' the lawyer observed. But then he saw the suspicious frown that Jud Harris was wearing and added hastily, 'Business partners, that is.'

'Of course,' said Maryanne as though she really might have had other ideas. She looked at Clem, smiled in a way that set his hopes rising and continued, 'Strictly business.'